CHTHONIC MATTER

A DARK FICTION QUARTERLY

SPRING 2023

Edited by

C.M. Muller

CHTHONIC MATTER
A Dark Fiction Quarterly

Volume 1, Issue 1

Typeset & Edited by C.M. Muller

© 2023 by Contributors

Fonts: "Night" & "Cormorant"

Cover art: Design Projects (via Shutterstock)

www.chthonicmatter.wordpress.com

CONTENTS

LOVE IS A GHOST YOU SEE WITH YOUR HEART

Luciano Marano

Beliefs differ, as with everything else. But I've read extensively on the subject and understand many experts insist that places cannot be haunted, only people. We make our own ghosts, they say, or bring them along with us, trailing in our wake like shed skin cells or the lingering smell of some psychic perfume.

Nevertheless, I am certain it's our *house* that is haunted.

I don't believe I'd merit such attention from you, darling. Not even now, after everything that happened. No, it's certainly our house you're haunting. It took too long for us to find and you loved it too much to let a little thing like death make you give it up. We paid more than we'd planned, but it was your dream house and you had to have it.

So I think you'd probably slam doors and rearrange furniture whether I still lived there or not.

Pretty good start, right?

Well, hold tight. It only gets creepier.

Scary stories are my favorite, both to read and to write. People don't often think of horror as being helpful, but I believe that's unfair. I believe it's through horror stories we come to know ourselves better.

I used to work primarily as a journalist, which means I wrote scary stories of a very different sort—but those horrors were never my fault. I didn't start the house fires. I didn't cause the car wrecks. I never even forced anybody to read the newspaper. But those scary stories were helpful (or at least informative).

Some people will always wonder at the appeal of horror fiction, though. My wife, for instance, she can't stand the sensation of being afraid. She doesn't like rollercoasters and she hates scary movies. And she's not alone.

Why, these people ask, would you want to read or watch something fake that was made up just to frighten you?

But the horror genre has proven perpetually popular, even (and sometimes especially) in times of uncertainty and turmoil. And I think that is because, in its own way, horror is reassuring.

I DON'T MIND the things you do, darling, really I don't. Break more plates, I'll clean up the mess and replace them. Shred the wallpaper if you like. I never cared for the pattern you picked. Tear all the books off the shelves and pile them in the center of the room. Most of them were yours anyway. Enjoy yourself, by all means. You always did prefer the company of books over me.

I hope you can see I've done my best to keep everything just like it was—the way you insisted it had to be. You always said I didn't listen, but see how carefully I replaced the books in the exact order you had them?

Remember how you used to get on my case about forgetting to clean the bathroom? Well, go ahead and make the walls bleed again, baby! I've got plenty of bleach and all the time in the world.

Did you notice that I kept your office exactly as you left it? Your desk and laptop, your notebooks and file cabinets bursting with new stories, they're all safe and sound in your favorite part of the house. The place where you spent countless hours making up fake adventures about imaginary people. People you loved more than me.

When I hear you clicking away on the keyboard now, it's almost like nothing has changed. I never saw you that much before.

Ah yes, the beloved tropes of the 'haunted house' story—timeless, universal perfection. Horror gives us many such useful metaphors through which we can visualize, articulate, and confront our anxieties. We may never cure cancer, but we can sure stake the hell out of some vampires! Terrorists are legion and can strike anywhere, anytime. But Michael Myers is just one guy, and he only kills people in that one little Illinois town—and always on the same day!

Scary stories give us hope without sugarcoating the odds. They tell us everything isn't going to be okay—and that's okay! Horror allows for optimism, but never forgets where the exits are. And I think that makes the happy endings, when they do come around, all the more valuable.

There is a legend in the annals of pop culture that while filming The Shining, Stanley Kubrick threw one of his famous tantrums and called Stephen King, in a rage, to vent. It was the middle of the night and King was hundreds of miles away, asleep. But he answered the phone and Kubrick reportedly said something like, 'It's no good, Steve. This story isn't scary. If the hotel is haunted, there really are ghosts. If there really are ghosts, death is not the end. It's comforting.'

History doesn't tell us King's exact response—I like to imagine it was a variation of, 'Who the hell is this?'—but Kubrick's theory got me thinking about ghosts being a comfort.

After all, a haunted house isn't such a bad place to live if your worst fear is being alone.

IT'S AUTUMN AGAIN, finally, your favorite season.

Today, I raked the leaves that fell from the big tree in the backyard. The one you named for some Tolkien character (you're such a nerd!) and in which I carved our initials, which you said was a stupid thing to do. The one underneath which we once had a picnic on your favorite blanket. The one beside which, alone in the middle of the night, I buried you.

Funny enough, it was a wedding present, the kitchen knife I used to finally touch your heart.

I used to worry that I wouldn't survive your absence. I tried taking an interest in your writing, but you said I was smothering you. I tried giving you space, but you said I was ignoring you. I tried to explain myself and you, half present as always, nodded and pretended to hear, but really you were off somewhere in your head, busy with dreams of imaginary people and fake worlds.

But I had dreams too, darling. Smaller than yours, it's true. Less fantastic, maybe, but they were mine and they mattered and you never listened.

But I think you're listening now.

You heard me tell the police I didn't know where you were—and that night the bedroom windows shattered.

You heard me say I had no idea why your car was parked near the bridge, although, come to think of it, you were acting rather depressed lately—and from every faucet poured black sludge reeking of decay.

You heard me tell everyone there was no new work, that my brilliant and eccentric husband emptied his files and wiped his computer before he disappeared—and the water in my aquarium boiled, killing all the fish.

Yes, I think you're listening to me now.

Try to remember it's only a story, just something a writer made up. I wouldn't be doing my job if you weren't a little uneasy at this point. There are no such things as ghosts, probably. But I actually think writers are like ghosts to the people who love us and live with us—often more presence than present.

You feel us there, just out of sight or in the next room, but you can't communicate with us (especially not when we're on a deadline). And if you do catch a glimpse of us, sitting in the corner or while passing each other in the kitchen, it can be impossible to really reach us. Even when we're physically with you, part of us is always elsewhere. Back in the world we've invented, agonizing over our precious sentences, or standing off to the side, observing the moment and considering how we might best depict it on paper later.

I'm a lucky guy. My wife never begrudges me the time I spend alone, obsessing about people who don't exist and events that will never happen. She doesn't get mad when I'm distracted by a story idea and didn't hear what she just said. Twice. And lately I can't help but wonder, if the situation were reversed, if I could be half as kind and selfless. It keeps me up at night, wondering about that. You see, I'm afraid that I know the answer.

We play with fear in order to master it. And fear, in turn, teaches us about ourselves. And while I like to think I'm a decent guy—does anybody ever really believe they're a bad person?—I work closely with fear every day, so I think I might know myself a little too well.

And I have doubts . . .

I STILL WORRY that I might not survive your absence. Lucky for me, you don't seem inclined to depart just yet.

Yes, I see you there, darling. And I caught a glimpse of you on the stairs the other day. You move much more quickly now, but not quickly enough to hide from me. I saw you lurking in the corner of the bedroom, too, just as I was torn from sleep after the windows shattered. I saw you behind me in the mirror when I wiped away the steam after my shower.

Muddy footprints in the hall. Cruel words—your words, I know them very well—scratched into my stomach. A dark figure in the shadow of our tree that seems to float above the ground. A deathly pale hand sliding out from the pile of leaves, finger beckoning me to come a little closer. Kitchen knives impaled into the wall.

The phone rings constantly, but when I pick it up there is never anybody there.

Maybe the experts are right and it's people who are haunted, not places. If that's true, maybe someday we'll get to haunt each other. Maybe we already are?

Or maybe I'm the one who's right. Years from now a new family will live here and have picnics in the yard, rake the leaves, arrange their books on the shelves, and try their best to ignore the strange happenings. Maybe they'll even joke about ghosts.

I think they'll tell jokes and learn to live with the things we do to each other or they'll move. Because it's our house, darling, and it always will be. And our house is haunted.

I wouldn't have it any other way.

LUCIANO MARANO is an award-winning author, photographer, and journalist. His short fiction has appeared in numerous anthologies, including *Year's Best Hardcore Horror*, *The Best New Weird Horror*, *Monsters, Movies & Mayhem* (winner: Colorado Book Award), and *Crash Code* (nominee: Splatterpunk Award), among others, as well as *Nightscript*, *Pseudopod*, and *Horror Hill*. A trilogy of werewolf novellas, *The Ambush Moon Cycle*, is now available. His reporting, written and photographic, has earned a number of industry awards, and he was twice named a Feature Writer of the Year by the Washington Newspaper Publishers Association. A U.S. Navy veteran originally from rural western Pennsylvania, he now resides near Seattle. (www.luciano-marano.com)

THE DEAD RADIO BROADCASTS

Charles Wilkinson

Peter Reginald was surprised to find the dead man's house full of radios. And not only where he might have expected to come across them: next to the armchair in the sitting-room, on the bedside table, in the kitchen not so far from the stove. Five were stacked in the warming cupboard, and others reclined on blankets and sheets. Not a single chair had been placed by the dining-room table, the surface of which was home to at least twenty types of radio, ranging from the latest digital models and tiny transistors to a wireless most probably dating from before the second war.

Outside, the sky was overcast, a uniform, ice-grey block. The little light that filtered through the window brought only a dull sheen to the silvery dust covering every object in the room, as if the whole world were frozen an hour before an all-day dusk. He switched on the nearest radio. Not a sound. The batteries were dead, but he twiddled the dial. Nothing, except for when he turned it off . . . a faint click like an insect flexing its legs.

Any heating in the house must been turned off long before a neighbor alerted the police, which resulted in the discovery of his former colleague's decomposed corpse. How hard it was to imagine there had ever been any warmth here. The chill seemed immemorial, as if built into the brickwork.

Peter tried to recall the last occasion he'd seen Walter Brown. At a leaving party? They'd both served the company for over thirty years and retired at the same time. Walter, who worked in the accounts, had always been so self-effacing it was strange for him to be the center of attention. Not that he tried to milk the occasion. His acceptance speech, when the carriage clock was presented to him, was both laconic and barely audible. Perfunctory applause followed. He'd be forgotten less than five minutes after he'd walked out of the door. Indeed, Peter had never spared him so much as a single thought until the chairman of Taylor and Griffin phoned the previous week.

"Ah, Peter," he heard Douglas Pedryck-Hall boom. "I'm afraid Walter Brown's dead."

"Oh, when did this happen?"

"A week or so ago. Anyhow, the point is this: a will has been found and you're one of the executors. I've just been contacted by his solicitor. Brown gave the firm as your address."

"But Brown . . . and I . . . we were hardly close."

"He wasn't close to anyone, was he? But he must have felt closer to you than the rest of us. Otherwise, he wouldn't have picked you as his executor. Be that as it may, there's a considerable amount of money at stake here. The man must have spent barely a fraction of his salary for decades, unless he had some source of private income."

"He seemed the parsimonious type, I admit."

"He left half of the money to the firm's benevolent fund and the other half to someone nobody has ever heard of. And now comes the difficult part: there's a codicil to the will stating that we can't claim our share until after the other beneficiary receives his cut."

"And his name is?"

"I can't recall. The solicitor will fill you in. But here's what we want you to do. Go down to the village where Brown lived and see if you can find out anything about the other fellow, the elusive executor *what's-his-name*. What a minute! Meldrum, yes, that's it."

"I'm rather busy at the moment."

"Oh come on, Reginald! You don't *have* to play golf every day of the week. And there will be something in it for you. A small amount for acting as an executor. Not that much, I'm afraid, but you won't go completely unrewarded."

A WEEK AFTER this conversation, Peter arrived late in the afternoon at the unprepossessing little village, hardly more than a hamlet,
where Walter had retired. Consisting of not much more than an un-
loved church marooned in an overgrown graveyard, a garage with a
two-pump petrol station in the forecourt and a pub that appeared
shut, it was hard to understand what had drawn Walter to the place,
especially as the property he'd purchased was undistinguished. A
squat cottage covered in yellow stucco, its diamond-paned windows
designed to admit light grudgingly, it stood in a dank garden dec-
orated with dripping, slack-leafed shrubberies. Peter had booked
himself into a bed and breakfast five miles away.

There was no point in trying to solve the riddle of the radios.
What he needed was to find the paperwork that would give him some
clue as to the whereabouts of the other executor, a Mr. T.S. Meldrum,
who was not known at the address the solicitors had provided.

Peter glanced around the sitting-room, a space small enough to
have served as a snug. No fireplace, no paintings on the wall and only
a solitary wooden chair by way of furniture. There was no desk on
the ground floor. None of the tables had drawers. Perhaps he'd find
Walter's study on the upper storey. The light from the single bulb
above him was yellowish, as if stained with urine.

Just as he reached the landing, Peter became aware of the rasp of radio noise; then the crackle of static, followed by a whine, as if someone were trying to tune in to the right frequency. This sound was soon replaced by a sizzle, behind which a voice could be heard, although the individual words were indistinct. Upstairs, there were only three rooms. The first had an old-fashioned, rust-stained bath, marked green-brown by a dripping tap. The second consisted of a single bed without so much as a lamp or a bedside table. The noise had to be coming from the third room. He pushed the door open. At first, it was hard to know if he'd chanced upon a radio cemetery or the place where they were to have been repaired. Over a hundred of them were spread out on the floor, the window sills, and on top of a chest of drawers. Many were in a state of disrepair, their backs off, displaying the glint of electrical innards. Others had twisted antennae or broken dials. A few were only discernible as shapes beneath grey snowfalls of dust. Every make that Peter had heard of was represented: Hacker, Roberts, Sony, Revel, Roxo, Revo, Philips, Fidelity, Grundig, Bose, Bush . . . and even what looked like a vintage valve radio. It was difficult to ascertain the direction of the hiss of static and the ghostly, faraway voice. As soon as he stretched out his hand to the nearest Hacker that seemed to be in good order, the sound stopped.

PETER ABANDONED THE search for Walter's papers. His former colleague seemed to have kept no records of any kind. Not so much as a utility bill or a solitary postcard from a friend abroad. At present, the only path worth pursuing appeared to be to inquire in the village. If Mr. Meldrum was a local man, someone must have heard of him.

A few wispy clouds were now visible, slightly paler than the smooth grey shell of sky enclosing the downcast afternoon, effectively shielding the village from the slightest prospect of sun. His first plan of action was to ask at the Post Office, but then he recalled that there wasn't one. No cars were parked in the forecourt of The Gaunt Shepherd. The pub's windows had been shuttered from the inside, which created the conceit of the building having been blinded by cataracts. He would have to inquire at the petrol station. The garage door was open. Peter peered into the petrol-scented murk and was able to make out two legs protruding from under the chassis of a puce-colored saloon car. A tinny transistor radio played a pop song from the 1950s.

"Excuse me!" No response. Peter walked over to the radio and switched it off. "Excuse me! I wonder if you could . . . "

A figure in stained brown overalls wriggled out from under the car. The man wore his unkempt hair long at the sides. His features were shiny with sweat and axle grease.

"What can I do for you, mate?" the man asked, looking up and evidently reluctant to abandon his prostrate position.

"I'm looking for a Mr. T.S. Meldrum."

"And you are?"

"I'm a former colleague of Walter Brown, and I'm trying—"

"A colleague but no friend, is that what you're telling me?"

"We weren't especially close, but he was a long-standing employee of the company for which we both worked. I expect you'll know that he died recently . . . "

"That's what they were saying in The Shepherd on Saturday night. But answer me this! Have you seen him laid out?"

For a moment, Peter had an image of a boxer flat out on the canvas, his opponent dancing away from him, hands aloft in triumph.

"Sorry?"

"Laid out proper. In a Chapel of Rest, like?"

"No, but that's not relevant. It's Meldrum I'm looking for. As to Brown's death, I'm perfectly prepared to accept his solicitor's word on the matter. Have you heard of this Meldrum?"

The man propped himself up on his elbows. "Might have. People have names around here, you know. And Meldrum is one of them."

"Do you know where I might find him?"

"Ask in The Shepherd."

"The place looks to be closed."

"It's Friday, isn't? It'll open at six-thirty sharp. Always has, always will. But careful what you say about Brown in there. Respected, he was. Knew his radios inside out. See that one there? The one that you turned off without asking? That was one of his. Gave it to me for next to nothing and it still works a treat."

"As I said, it's Meldrum I'm looking for," Peter replied.

The radio started up the instant Peter reached the entrance. He swung round. The man was back underneath the car, his legs sticking out as before. For all his lugubrious manner, the mechanic must have been surprising agile to switch on the radio and return to his previous position so swiftly.

As Peter strode across the road, he recalled that he had failed to take the number of the taxi which had brought him from the bed and breakfast. The prospect of spending the night in the cottage was unappealing. He could always telephone for a cab from The Shepherd at some point in the evening, but it would be all too easy to forget. Then he saw the familiar shape of a red telephone box on a grass verge close to the pub. A local taxi firm might well have left their card in there.

As he opened the door of the booth, he was assailed by the intermixed scents of cigarettes and urine. Gritty glass crunched beneath his feet. He picked up the receiver and heard the dialing tone. Outside, a youth with a crew cut walked along the street, a transistor radio pressed to his right ear. A card had been wedged into one of the few windowpanes still intact. As he tried to retrieve it, there was resistance from bubble-gum, a string of which stretched out, leaving a sticky residue on his fingers. It was still light enough to be able to read: UNDERWORLD TAXIS, *Terrific for Local Trips and Destinations Beyond.* The name, with its implications of gangsterism, was odd, but he might as well try them. In fact, weren't they the firm that had brought him to the village? The phone call was picked up at once by someone who coughed until the phlegm in his chest cracked.

"And so," said a guttural voice, recovering, "you're asking to be taken across?"

"I'm not sure I grasp your meaning. Across what?"

"From one side to another."

"Well, I suppose so. Although that's a strange way to put it. I want to be collected from outside The Gaunt Shepherd at closing time, and dropped off at Far Bank Guest House."

"Someone will be there, Mr. Reginald. At 11:00 o'clock sharp. And oh, cash only, no cards."

"That will be fine."

"And no notes, just coins."

"Well, I'm sure whoever is behind the bar will be able to oblige with change."

AS HE WAITED in the cottage for opening time, he asked himself what could possibly have persuaded Walter Brown to appoint him as an executor. For the last twenty years they'd had very little to do with each other. The only time the man's name came up was if it was suggested at a board meeting, when the post of Head of Finance came up, that as the longest-serving accountant Walter should be appointed. Peter always successfully opposed this. Whilst he was prepared to accept that Brown was capable enough, he appeared to be the living proof that members of that profession were dullness perfected. There were other well-qualified people in accounts with a little more pizzazz, surely? If Brown became a director of the firm, he'd have to meet real people instead of totting up rows of figures and working out percentages. And his dress sense hadn't altered in thirty years—still the same symphony in beige, putty colors that matched the pallor of his hangdog features and frameless glasses. The only thing that had altered was his coiffure, the progression to absolute baldness that commenced with a receding hairline in his twenties before becoming a pronounced widow peak in his early thirties. The unflattering comb-over was a disaster of his middle years. By his fifties only a few thin grey strands persisted. He wondered if Walter had ever become aware of the implacability of Peter's opposition to his promotion.

What his colleague could not have forgotten was the way that he'd been driven out of the Masons Arms, the inn across the road they'd both frequented as young employees. Brown drank half pints instead of pints, he never put his hand in his pocket to buy a round, and contributed nothing to the conversation. After a few months of this, Peter was one of those who retaliated, always within earshot of everyone, with a barrage of drollery and barbs. Would Walter buy a drink before or after the Second Coming? What make of padlock did Walter use to secure his wallet? Was Walter's stinginess innate or had he done a degree course in Applied Parsimony? After a week or so of this, his colleague was never seen in the Masons Arms again. But if what was happening was Walter's idea of retribution, it seemed perfectly in accord with the man's apparent mildness of manner. Yes, Peter was being very slightly inconvenienced, but nothing more. If he secured the money for the Benevolent Fund, and a small emolument for himself into the bargain, who would deny his time had been well spent?

AT 6:25 SOMEONE opened the shutters of The Gaunt Shepherd to reveal a brassy glow tinged with red, a shade between a warmish welcome and the infernal. A minute later came the rasp of a bolt being drawn back. The heavy wooden door groaned open, and Peter stepped into a coffin-shaped room. The bar was in front of him, the furthest end of which formed a triangular nook, beamed and with low wooden benches on either side. The other end was dominated by an open fire with oak settles. The not unpleasing interior was compromised by a collection of skulls kept in glass cabinets alongside the wall closest to the door. Peter inspected them. It was perfectly possible that most were of ovine origin, but a few were undoubtedly not.

The man behind the bar was tall and saturnine, and he wore what appeared to be a peasant's smock. Was this place supposed to be a 'themed' pub? There were no sickles on the wall or grainy black and white photographs of fields with stooks or sheep. And no picture of an eponymous shepherd, gaunt or otherwise. An ancient wireless positioned at the far end of the bar was playing, but the volume had been turned down so low that nothing could be heard through the static except the sound of two voices, arguing apparently, although there was no discerning the sense of what was being said.

"I'm looking for a Mr. T.S. Meldrum."

The barman had dark eyes set in deep sockets. He studied Peter for a long a time before answering mildly: "That's fine. No one here is going to stop you if that's what you're minded to do."

"Do you know of a Mr. Meldrum? I'm trying to find him."

"You've already said that," he replied, his tone tetchier. "That was established almost as soon as you walked through door."

Perhaps he'd inadvertently adopted the wrong approach. He should have a bought a drink first and then, after a moment or two of general conversation, inquired after Meldrum. Whilst his pint was being poured, Peter asked the man if he was the landlord.

"I am."

"And how long have you kept this inn?"

"Twenty years."

"And so you knew Walter Brown."

"Half-pint Walter? He stood where you're standing every Friday and Saturday night for half an hour. Had his half pint and then left."

"So you know he died?"

"Well, he doesn't come in any longer, does he?"

"He was keen on radios, I believe."

As the landlord looked at Peter, there was a flash of indignation in his brown-black eyes. "Everyone has a radio round here. There's nothing wrong with that, is there?"

"No, not at all. Listening to the radio is an admirable way of passing the time. But he seems to have owned quite a few of them."

"Walter was a real 'radio man.' You'd think a set was dead, fit for nothing but the scrap heap, but give it to Walter and he'd coax a tune out it. Get it to say the shipping forecast. He had a wonderful way with them, did Walter."

"And Meldrum . . . did he have a similar affinity with—"

"A pint of mild and a bottle of pale ale."

A man with a cratered mauve moon of a face and claw-like hands huge as a mechanical digger's, in one of which he was holding a steel dog bowl, loomed into view next to Peter. The pub was becoming crowded, and it would be some time before he could re-capture the landlord's attention. He picked up his pint and made his way to one of the settles by the fire. A moment later he was joined by the large man, now accompanied by a ragged, black-and-white sheepdog.

"You don't mind if I put myself here," said the man, after he had already sat down, spreading his enormous thighs so that he occupied more than half of the seat. "There's room for a little one, eh?"

Peter watched while the man opened the pale ale and poured the contents into the dog bowl.

"I've not seen you here before, have I?"

"No. I'm a former colleague of Walter Brown. I've just been—"

"I hope you're not going to clear the house out. There's a lot of very important kit in there."

"If you're referring to the radios, yes, there are a great many of them. But as they are mostly in poor repair, I can't see that they'd be of great value."

The man swung towards Peter. His eyes were bloodshot, the whites lemon-yellow but filigreed with veins, some of which had burst. "You're not thinking of moving anything . . . some of that equipment is very delicate. The last thing the village wants is a bloke who thinks he knows it all coming in from outside and fiddling with the frequencies, buggering the bandwidth about, causing some kind of electromagnetic meltdown."

"Actually, it's not the radios that I'm interested in. I'm searching for a man named Meldrum. A friend of Walter, I believe."

"Walter and Meldrum pals? I've never seen them together. Not in all the time I've lived in the village."

"But he came in here? Meldrum?"

"Yes, he did. Sometimes. But Walter was a 6:30 on the dot man. Meldrum only ever just made it in time for last orders."

"And what sort of man was he, this Meldrum?"

"*This* Meldrum," said the big man, matching his voice to Peter's middle-class tones. "That's not how we refer to other people round-about here. Now, if you don't mind, I'll fetch my dog another Pale Ale."

A new group of drinkers arrived. With their green-and-brown tweed jackets, thick-soled footwear, flat caps, and wind-scoured, rubicund faces, they immediately dominated the space by the bar. Something about them was redolent of an earlier era: one wore plus-fours, several had their trousers tucked into their thick woolen socks. The man making the most noise had a bright red feather tucked into the hatband of his fedora. A shooting party, no doubt. It was plain that Peter wasn't going to get anything more out of the big man, who was joshing with the hunters and laughing with ex-orbitant gusto. The dog staggered woozily to its feet and whimpered in the direction of its owner. Peter decided he might as well place himself somewhere with more elbow room before the remaining seats were taken.

By ten to eleven, business had begun to thin. Only the hunter in the fedora and the big man were still at the bar. Next to the fireside settle, the dog was either asleep or in an ale-induced stupor. A line of empty bottles stood by its bowl. The landlord called last orders. There was no sign of anyone who might have been Meldrum. Peter decided to wait outside for his taxi. Moments later, the hunter and the big man, followed by his unsteady animal, came out. Peter looked at his watch: no sign of the taxi, which was over twenty minutes late. Livid at finding himself stuck in the village, he tried the front door. Fortunately, it was unlocked.

The landlord was collecting glasses from the tables.

"What do you want? The bar's shut."

"I ordered a cab, but it hasn't turned up."

"Which company?"

"Underground Taxis. I want to get back to The Far Shore Guest House."

The landlord laughed. "That lot would happily take you *from* the guest house, but there's no way they're going to bring you back."

"Are there any other firms?"

"What, at this time of night? You won't be going anywhere, I'm afraid."

"And you don't do accommodation?"

"No. Show yourself out. I want to lock up."

Outside, Peter stared at a full moon imprisoned by thin chains of cloud. Somewhere in the dark, a radio was being tuned, scratching from channel to channel, a single word or a bar of music audible for a second before being obliterated. There was no alternative to spending the night at the cottage. As he was about to step onto the road, a grey figure, his head bowed, slipped past. Was this Meldrum? He hurried off in pursuit of what he could now see was a man wearing a mackintosh.

"Mr. Meldrum! You wouldn't by any chance . . . "

The man accelerated without lengthening his stride, let alone breaking into a run. Were his feet even in contact with the ground? What surprised Peter was that his quarry was on course for the entrance to the cottage. But moments later, on reaching his goal, instead of knocking at the door, he started to melt into the stucco. His mackintosh dissolved in less than a minute, followed by his trousers and upturned feet. The back of his head, surviving for a while as a blob of impasto, was the last of him to fade through the paintwork and into the mortar.

THE SOUND OF VOICES in the street awoke Peter at seven-thirty in the morning. As there was not so much as an armchair, let alone a sofa, in the sitting-room, there'd been no alternative to sleeping in Walter's bed. To slip between the dead man's sheets in nothing more than a pair of boxer shorts proved disconcerting. The damp linen and distressed mattress, which must have been in service for three or four decades, still held the shape of Walter's body, which made sleep difficult.

Of course, there'd been no sign of anyone else in the house the previous night. What had occurred was almost sufficient to over-turn his long held skepticism of the supernatural. This morning, however, he was inclined to attribute what he'd seen to drink. Admittedly, he'd felt entirely lucid at the time, but he'd been im-bibing with metronomic regularity from the hour the inn opened to last orders. A dry mouth, leaden skull, and pervasive queasiness were the proof of it. Nevertheless, his mind must have been working hard overnight because in spite of a whole body hangover, he'd worked out what Walter had planned. As soon as he'd had a strong black coffee, he'd phone the firm and let them know. The news wouldn't be well-received, but at least no one would have to waste any more time unravelling the conundrum that was Mr. Meldrum.

As Peter began to get dressed, he realized the voices he'd thought he'd heard on the street were coming from the ground floor. He went to the top of the stairs and listened intently. He couldn't hear what was being said, but two men were arguing. He slipped downstairs. There was no one there. After five minutes of investigation, he tracked the disturbance down to a radio in the kitchen that he'd assumed was dead, for the back had been taken off and there were no batteries. Had someone plugged it in at the mains? Impossible. There was no lead. He turned up the volume. It took him a moment to recognize the speaker, for the voice was distorted by rage, but what he was hearing was Walter, screaming obscenities with the virulence of man a trapped in a hell made for two. Peter flung the radio to the ground and then jumped on it, stamped on it, spat on it, kicked it around the room until it disintegrated. Open-mouthed, he stood for a while breathing heavily, waiting for the return of silence.

As soon as it was nine o'clock, Peter rang the office from the phone outside the pub and asked to be put through to Pedryck-Hall.

"Sorry, Douglas. Bad news, I'm afraid. I'm pretty certain that Walter Brown was Mr. Meldrum. Local lore has it that Meldrum lived in these parts. He was seen in the pub, but never appeared at the same time as Brown. No one will admit it, but they must have been one and the same man."

"But why on earth would anyone go along with something so absurd as that?"

"I don't know. Perhaps it's a private joke at the expense of outsiders. But there's also a kind of cult here, which I don't completely understand."

"A cult? What sort of cult?"

"It's to do with radios. Oddly enough, Walter was widely respected as some sort of radiophonic guru. No doubt that's another reason people went along with his fantasy."

"So this means that Brown, in effect, left the money to himself, and since he's dead and has no known relatives . . . his estate will go to the Crown."

"Yes. You could try checking the births and deaths register to see if there ever has been a T.S. Meldrum with the right dates. But I'm certain I'm correct."

Peter put the phone down and walked back over the road. The house was filled with the uproar of hundreds of radios rapidly coming to life one after the other, a hubbub of voices, complaining, raging—and all of them Walter's, though the sounds were unsynchronized and the meaning of the message merged into a Babel of imprecations washed by waves of static. He became aware of a second voice, imprecise initially; then raised until it became recognizable as his own. His tone was pleading at first, that of a man clamoring to avert a catastrophe. Peter raced out the house and into the street. Wasn't it supposed to be morning? The scene in front of him was suffused with a sense of the day's impending closure, the last moments of light before the dark.

He hammered on the door of The Gaunt Shepherd. No answer. As the last blow echoed and then faded, he became aware of a stupendous silence inside the building. The disturbance was still concentrated on the cottage, growing louder and louder, accelerating towards a crescendo, the sound almost a physical force now, as though skidding on the airwaves towards him. A workman walked past, apparently oblivious to the sonic beldam. That such a pandemonium was not audible on their side of the street seemed impossible. Then the voices resumed more clearly, but they were inside him now—Walter's first: every word he said was distinct, laden with acrimony and grievance. Peter listened to a litany of grudges, a lifetime's worth of resentments and humiliations. And he heard himself responding, imploring Walter to put an end to his complaints. The clamor of the dead radios decreased. Soon all Peter was aware of were the voices inside him. Somehow he had become the final receiver, the recipient of the airwaves and the fixed frequency.

But he knew that the immensity of this moaning and his power-less replies were being played and re-played, as if on a loop that would last for every day that he remained alive—and longer.

CHARLES WILKINSON's collections of strange tales and weird fiction, *A Twist in the Eye* (2016), *Splendid in Ash* (2018), *Mills of Silence* (2021), and *The Harmony of the Stares* (2022), appeared from Egaeus Press. Eibonvale Press published his chapbook of weird stories, *The January Estate*, in 2022. Individual stories have appeared in *Nightscript, Black Static, Bourbon Penn, Shadows & Tall Trees, Supernatural Tales*, and other publications. He lives in Wales. More information can be found at his website: www.charleswilkinsonauthor.com.

THE SONG OF A CROW

Eygló Karlsdóttir

Eyes glistening with old horror, dead. Insects crawling inside. A familiar grin on his face.

The sun shone, but it was cold. The black sand underneath my feet felt ominous, hazardous, and unsafe. I leaned down, expecting the vision in the sand to fade before my eyes, expecting it to be one of those things you see in the arctic desert after long exposure to the elements. A deadweight delusion, a monstrous mirage.

For some reason I expected to see the back porch staircase before me, instead of the skeleton.

The crow sat on a pole in the distance, glaring. I had questioned the bird's existence in the past, questioned reality. It was a way to survive the journey. One foot in front of the other and I would find the place. All I had to do was endure the vision in the sands and the cold. The unearthly desert, black obsidian cliffs in the distance, dark sand as far as the eye could see. It held no life except the occasional bird, and a dead or dying tree, raising its branches up towards the sky in a final prayer.

I leaned down. The dead man looked up at me, at the darkening sky above, and for a moment I thought he was nodding. Then a beetle scuttled from underneath his chin, big and black. It stopped on the man's collar, seemed to contemplate what to do next, its little-big head swerving, and then it scuttled down the man's torso and vanished underneath his arm.

I shuddered, looked up at the laughing crow. The screeches loud and terrifying.

"Shut up," I told the bird and rose to my feet.

Leaving the dead man behind me was easy enough, but the image of the beetle, the hollow eyes and the crow's laughter stayed with me. I kept heading for the mountains far in the distance. There was nothing else to do. Only a drowned witch could help, and I knew where to find her. The bird had told me as much.

Skepticism filled my bones at first, of course. You know how it is. An Icelandic girl has a premonition. A volcano bursts, first slowly, almost peacefully but then with accelerated fervor and ferocity. It threatened the city, and a small town on the coast. The crow came to me in a dream first, the laughter echoing through a moonlit night, the sea struggling against a terrible storm. I sat on a stone, staring at the crow. Then it started talking.

"Dead or dying," the bird said.

I woke up in a fit, sweaty, struggling, but paid no heed to the warning. It was just a dream, until it wasn't, and I really did sit on the stairs, this time in my own sheltered backyard and the crow sat on a nearby branch. It screeched a second warning, the words echoed from beyond the crow's own body, as if it came from another world, from another time.

I told my husband. He helped me contact a doctor. I was lost or losing it.

The nurses told me to let it go, said I was calm and collected and that I could see a psychiatrist. They told me that I would be fine, that I was in no grave danger, that my issues weren't severe. I was to go home, ignore the bird and do my best to go on with my life. They basically told me to walk it off.

Anxiety ruled my life for the time to come. I went on, though it was always as if something was missing in my life, as if I'd suddenly lost my connection with the real world. I often felt as if I'd forgotten something. I felt sad and alone despite my husband's reassurances.

Then the impossible happened.

The crow sat on a windowsill outside my window, first mild, looking at me, crowing. Slowly, its words returned, harsher now.

"Hurry, hurry," the crow cawed, and I knew I had to go. I had to find her, the witch, a drowned witch. Which seems like such a contradiction. A drowned witch is a dead witch. The thought came to me haphazardly, as if from someone else, from up above. I heard birds talk. I knew this wasn't sane, so I ignored the bird and my own intuition and watched the sunset echo in the red sky long after midnight. The volcano was angry and getting angrier.

The next day it was too late. The little town by the shore had to be evacuated, people lost their homes, two died. My neighbor was the one to tell me. He had a solemn face, but his eyes burned with fervor and for an instant I was sure he was the witch. I pulled myself together, reminded myself of how reality works and managed a smile.

Later, the bird shook its head at me, told me to go to the desert. Whispers of something echoed through me, hollow, empty, and atrocious. I drove to the south, far away from the volcano, far away from the pandemic and the city that I was sure the volcano would take next.

When I came to the black desert I started walking.

It wasn't until I saw the obsidian mountains that I realized I wasn't really in Iceland anymore. It wasn't until I saw the dead man in the ground that I realized I had been misled. The crow was a harbinger, but it wasn't the mountain that posed a problem. It was something else, something much more personal.

The walk through the desert was exhausting, cold, and dry. I had a water bottle, but there was no way to refill it until I came to the mountains, so I had to drink sparingly. I thought of looking to see if the dead man had any water with him, but the beetle creeped me out, as did the grotesque grin on his face, and so I walked away, leaving the bleary-eyed corpse behind me.

"Hurry, hurry," I heard the crow cry.

I did as it asked, and all the bird did was laugh.

"Worry, worry."

The winter was exhausting. Everything had gone wrong. Pandemic isolation, work related issues, depression along with the fear of the unknown bug sweeping the world. My marriage suffered. He was moody, dreary-eyed, drinking, but we hadn't been worse off than anyone else. We were just like everyone, affected but surviving, barely.

It would all be alright, in the end. I loved him. He loved me. A foggy future tantalizing in the distance, far away.

As the bird kept mocking me I felt the horror rise within me. This was folly. I had listened to a voice inside me. A voice that had lost its compass and now I roamed the landscape, hoping to find salvation in the madness. Reality was behind me.

I fled.

When I came to a slow brook I filled my water bottle, drank myself full. The air was clear, the evening full of stars. The red glow in the distance only matched by the burning aurora borealis, painting the sky in green and purple. I stared, listening to the crow whisper behind me.

"Glory, Glory," it cooed, mimicking a city dove.

I kept on walking until I stood by the roots of the smooth obsidian mountains. The image of the dead man haunted my memory, but I couldn't move forward. I had to find the drowned witch, and that meant finding an entrance to her dark cave.

The bird showed me the way. "Climb a cliff," it said.

My visions came to me clearly now, easily.

Obsidian cliffs are slippery, smooth, and perilous, but I climbed, finding a foothold until the platform evened out to reveal an opening in the mountain. Above the entrance a symbol had been carved into the wall. It was a humble daisy wheel, pretty in its simplicity.

Inside was a long corridor, and then light. I moved slowly, silently, entering the cave hall, lurking in the shadows, hoping for the best, fearing the worst.

"Stay away, slayer," the witch said. "The crow does you no favors."

I didn't say anything, just sat down on the floor. It was covered in soft hay. I found myself wondering how she got anything up to this place, deep in the mountain. She looked rowdy, pale, and dark-eyed. Her hair was in a knot, but grey strands had escaped. It looked like she was conducting electricity. I could see the sparkles flying from the tip of her hair, from her fingers.

The bird stayed outside. Invisible, but I found myself wondering if it was observing us, somehow.

"I think I've lost my mind," I told the witch. "I thought I—" I stopped talking, looked at her and wondered why she looked familiar.

"Quiet, girl," the woman said.

She put her hand on a scarf that lay on top of a chair that looked like it had been carelessly put together from branches, the top of it still reaching for the sky, like those dead trees in the desert. I shrugged and looked around. The place was full of small trinkets, skulls and bones, dry beetles, and crawling spiders.

I shivered.

"I just want to go home," I told her. "I just want things to return to normal, the way they were before—"

"Before what?" the witch asked, but it wasn't a real question. I knew that. She took a small glass bottle from a natural shelf by the fire that burned by the cave wall, and then she poured whatever was in it into a small pot. She stirred with her finger and licked it. The green liquid trickled down, spilled. Then she turned to me, cocked her head, and mumbled to herself. Her voice harsh and raspy.

"Lethe, she needs a drop from Lethe," she told herself. The bottle was small, looked like crystal, shining in the light from the fire.

"Do you even remember?" she asked, approaching me. She put a small glass with the green liquid in front of me and smiled. "Do you?"

I nodded. "It was better."

"Better? Better than what?"

I didn't answer, just stared at the green goo bubbling in the glass.

"Drink, it'll take a while to work," she said.

"What is it?"

"You came for my help, didn't you?"

"I'm going to die, people are going to die—" I looked at the cave entrance and wondered if it was even there. If it was real.

"The bird?" she asked.

I lifted the glass, then I drank it all. The liquid was bitter, tasted of spinach and of something else as well, something I didn't want to know about.

"Why are you here?" I asked her.

"Afterlife is a bitch," she said. "They drowned me, a witch. This is what I get."

"I'm sorry," I told her. But the indication rang in me, the implication alive in my bones, in my belly. I wanted to hurl. I wanted to vomit up the green liquid, but I couldn't. It had to stay down.

"Deadly," she said.

"What is? The thing I drank?"

"The bird." She grinned at me. "Farewell, dead girl," she said.

I wanted to ask her what she meant but couldn't muster up the words. Instead, I stumbled out of the cave. I just wanted to get away from her. I just wanted to get away, get back to the car and go home.

"Farewell, killer," I heard the echoes in my mind. Like the cawing of the incessant crow.

I saw the image of my husband before me. His brown eyes looking at me that way, like he loves me, like he cares for me. That look that had passed between us a thousand times and would a thousand more. Then his grin becomes wicked. It's not him, but the skull in the sand, glaring at me.

"You have a choice." I hear a voice. It's not the crow. "Learn the truth or try again."

I spun around and looked at the witch.

Her eyes, cold grey, like my own. Her demeanor soft, slow. I fell. Or I saw someone falling. I fell.

When I awoke, I was lying by my car. The ice floating in the lagoon, the black desert before me. The white slopes of the glacier in the distance, dark streaks painting the cold exterior. I felt a headache coming on and for an instant I wondered if it was from the brew the witch gave me.

Then reality dawned on me.

There was never any witch. Never any bird.

I got into my car and drove back to the city. The fiery gloom emanated from the mountain in the distance, lit up the night sky. The roads were lonely, the sky loud.

When I got home I ate a sandwich and drank a lot of water. My husband wasn't home. He was working late. I went to bed hoping everything would be normal when I woke up again. Hoping I wouldn't dream, hoping I wouldn't wake up with the anxiety looming in my chest, blooming. Breaking my spirit.

I hoped I wouldn't wake up to the chattering bird, or with the taste of spinach on my lips.

Have you ever seen sand seep through the hands of a dead man? It's as if you spend forever in that very moment, watching the sand slowly filter through the dead, frosted fingers. It looks like a macabre hourglass, counting the seconds lived, counting down till the end of time. Counting the passing of each moment, reminding you of one single horrendous accident.

When I woke up, the bird was cawing madly.

"Sorry, sorry," it told me.

I went to the kitchen, passing the porch door. It was painted black, crude streaks of rotten wood layered underneath, protruding. I ignored it. Ignored the stench. I got myself a cup of coffee and then I stood in front of it. The bird shouting its warning.

"Bury, bury."

I opened the door, and suddenly I was there again. In the black desert, looking at the sand bleeding through the dead man's fingers, and it all came back to me.

He stumbled down the stairs.

At the bottom of the staircase was the fine-grained sand, stained with blood. He lay there, eyes wide open, on the ground.

My husband.

The backyard tree reached for the sky, dead branches praying solemnly.

I stumbled to my knees, buried my face in my hands.

"Fury, fury," I heard the bird sing.

We argued.

His eyes stared up at me from their bed in the sand, the beetle scuttling underneath his chin. The palm of his hand full of sand.

"Pushing up the daisies," the bird twittered. "Blurry, blurry."

I felt the taste of spinach in my mouth, smelled the acid sulphur and knew the lava would soon drown everything, drown me.

"Hurry, hurry," the bird instructed.

I took his hand, still looking at the sand seeping between his fingers. Dark, dead sand. I lay down beside him, curled his hand around me and waited. I knew it was only a matter of time before the lava consumed me, and as I lay there I realized why the drowned witch had been so familiar.

She was me, and I was her, forever bound by the premonition-bird, that keeps us knowing. Binds us to our wicked deeds.

I pushed him down the stairs. I didn't mean to harm him, but he was teasing me, tickling me and he came too close to that nerve deep inside of me, that fragile thing that means I would have opened up my soul to him, opened up my heart. It was easier to let him fall, and so after catching his hand, he balanced there forever on top of the staircase, and then I let go and he fell.

Wasn't that what happened? He loved me. That must have been what happened.

Or was it I who fell? Was I the one who tumbled down the stairs? Cracked my skull? The dark sand counting the hours, pouring between my own dead fingers?

I fell.

The sand still pours before my eyes. I count the minutes, the hours, the days. The natural hourglass counting the moments before my last judgment. I was the one who fell, I was the one who let go, but he was the one who walked away, leaving me to rot. Leaving me to listen to the mumbling crow.

"Sorry, sorry."

EYGLÓ KARLSDÓTTIR was born and raised in Iceland but lives currently in the south of Sweden with her daughter and her dog. She enjoys photography, reading, and taking long walks in the forest. She is the author of the novellas *All the Dark Places* and *In His Mind, Her Shadow*, and has released the short story collections *Things The Devil Wouldn't Dream of And Other Stories* and *Seafood & Cocktails*. She has also had some success with getting stories into anthologies like *The Mammoth Book of Halloween Stories* and *Hex-Periments*, to name just two. For more information visit www.eyglo.info.

AMUSEMENT

Perry Ruhland

The infection, cruel as it became, seemed at first to be a gift to our long-stagnant town. It came first as a Ferris wheel, stout and sturdy, and from its lighted ring swung seven gondolas, each assigned a dulled color of the rainbow. Nobody had seen the wheel the night before, nor had anyone claimed to know of a carnival coming to town, but there it was, a vibrant flower bursting from a field of hollowed strip malls. Upon approaching the site, even early rising visitors were confronted with a crowded queue which zig-zagged out before the wheel. While waiting, guests would have ample opportunity to watch the bulb-rimmed wheel glow bright against the grey winter vault. It was a simple attraction; every minute or so a crowded gondola would land at the embankment on the wheel's underside. The gondola's doors would open (automatically—"a marvel of engineering"), its forgettable party would depart, and another would replace them. The doors would then close, and the gondola would rise, a minute hand running up towards the northern noon in reverse like a Hebrew clock. This circular motion would then be interrupted six times when the course of the ride would halt and, as the contents of the lower gondola were replaced, the others would sway like the dangling fruit of a gale-battered tree. In time the waiting guests would find themselves before the red-and-white-striped operating booth that stood at the foot of the wheel. The window to the booth was darkened to the point of total obscurity, rendering the station—and presumably, its attendant—invisible. Unfettered by the strangeness of the sight, and disastrously unbothered by the anonymity of the whole affair, the families would then board the attraction. They would experience a brief period of minor amusement marred only by a slight nausea that owed to the gondola's swaying. Then they would go home.

I did not see this manifestation firsthand. This strange episode was relayed to me by Antonio, a coworker at the shabby cafe where I was long employed. In many ways, Antonio was the sort of man I would generally avoid: boisterous, opinionated, prone to over-excitement and shaped by decades of following his every fleeting instinct. However, what we shared was more important than any incongruences of temperament, and that was a sneering distaste for the town which we begrudgingly called home. We'd spend our days complaining, and even when returning to our most well-worn objections we always found new curses for the lot: the slop-hungry denizens dozing through their days, the bumbling authorities herding us off a cliff, the tomblike grey that subsumed any potential character beneath its fungal stink, and most importantly, the knowledge that it was unlikely for anywhere else to be all that markedly better. But while our passions aligned, our methods of cultivation couldn't have been any more different. While I preferred to sow my hate from the comfort of my own apartment, lost in old books and aromatic teas, Antonio lived to stick his nose in the stink. This is how he came to tell me his tall tales of raving derelicts under the humpbacked bridge, spectral eyes that shone from the windows of a decrepit meat market, and now this amusement, which seemed at once his most preposterous and least foreboding invention.

"After all," I said, "it ran fine, it amused the kids, it'll leave in time. I don't quite see the harm. It's just a Ferris wheel."

"Ah-ah …" He wagged a calloused finger. "Were you not listening to me? It's not that this alien machine is the only new visitor to our town, but rather, it was the first. *Was* the first. Do you understand?"

"Sure," I said. "You mean to tell me that the Ferris wheel is only some herald for something worse, a 'preemptive tombstone to mark the chaos to come.' We've been here before."

"No, it's not that something is coming, but rather it has already come. The Ferris wheel was only its first manifestation. The second arrived just this morning. You haven't seen it?"

"Seen what?"

"Of course you haven't. Well, if a diversion in an abandoned lot is too far-fetched, I know you'd never believe this one. You'll just have to see it yourself. And don't give me that look—I'm not about to send you on some wild goose chase. You can find this one in your own backyard, so to speak. You know Holsten's, the whiskey bar on Mangrove Street?" he asked as if we hadn't, on multiple occasions, drank there together. "I thought you might. After your shift, you should give it a visit. Go and take a look at the offices across the street."

"And then?"

"And then you'll see where we're going."

IT WAS ONLY mid-afternoon when my shift ended, but the winter gloom had already banished the sun and transformed the streets into cold, dark gutters. I pictured the long walk ahead, shivering through twisted alleys and windswept plazas, frozen globules of snot clinging to my mustache. I supposed then that I could justify a drink or two.

As I headed towards the bar, any awareness of the grim temperature was blotted out by visions of warm amber pools. In just a manner of blocks I was fully immersed in my alcoholic fantasies, and it was only when I reached Mangrove Street that I faltered. A large crowd had congealed at the end of the inclined street, a mass of bodies clung tight around what I assumed must have been Antonio's offices. Although I could now feel the frost gnawing at my fingers, curiosity got the better of me: I put the drink on hold and joined the shivering crowd.

It was clear that the mass was huddled around the office building, although for what purpose I could not say—surely I'd passed the complex many times before and found it unremarkable. I tried to assess the scene from the back of the crowd, but all I could make out were occasional flashes of red light over covered heads and the gentle hum of some hidden calliope. It was cold, and I was curious, so despite my manners I shoved my way towards the front. The spectators moved without protest, their faces dull and sallow, gazes fixed ahead. Eventually I reached the tip, where the amorphous mass of people siphoned off into a zig-zagging queue, and it was there that I saw the spectacle. The building, that oppressive slab of grey, now sported a curious new addition. It was a carousel, an elevated platform that spun slowly to the tune of a tinny calliope, carrying on its current a set of gold-painted bars which skewered the backs of varicolored horses. It protruded from the building like a bright, prismatic tumor, sagging out hideously from the otherwise intact concrete wall, allowing only a wedge of its red-and-white-striped canopy to be visible. In an alarming flourish, the left side of the carousel had spilled into and entirely swallowed up the building's vestibule; I could almost see the horses turn behind the glass doors. With the entrance effectively blocked, it seemed the only purpose the three-story structure now served was to act as a receptacle for the carousel, which it fulfilled in its own clumsy way. Earlier, I had questioned Antonio's use of words like 'manifested' to describe the impromptu birth of the Ferris wheel in the north side of town, but now I understood: there was simply no way the aberration had been built by human hands.

Presently all of the carousel's horses were occupied, and as the platform spun a stream of parka-clad passengers would briefly appear out from the burrowed majority of the ride to bob before the crowd, then disappear back into the depths, only to appear again a short while later. Soon the calliope began to fade, and the carousel slowed to a halt, vibrant horses suspended mid-gallop. The riders who were visible to us riders-in-waiting dismounted and departed, and they were soon joined by those whose ride ended within the bowels of the building. And when the new riders mounted, I then noticed something I had until then neglected. Standing at the foot of the carousel was a stout red-and-white-striped booth, its window darkened to the point of total obscurity.

Holsten's was empty. This was not unusual for a weekday afternoon (not that I was an expert in such matters) but given the crowd which had amassed across the street, the bar seemed especially desolate. I hung my layers at the entrance and sat at the bar. Tomas, a stout man with bottle-cap glasses, greeted me with a plastic smile.

He poured my usual. The first sip restored feeling to my face, the rest was a luxury. The whole while Tomas stood on the other side of the counter, his face fixed in some exaggeration of a thoughtful frown, eyes aimed just past me as if to disguise his intention. He didn't have to try so hard—but still I said, with as little commitment as I could affect:

"Very strange out there."

"Mm…" He nodded. "Last night, when I was closing, there was nothing. It was just another building. And then this morning, there it was, spinning away. Music blaring, horses turning, that little booth just standing there. People have been lined up since the crack of dawn. Part of me thinks it's the same group riding again and again, but I can't say. They must love it. To wait out in the cold for so long, for something like that."

I shivered and finished my drink. Behind the frosted windows, the crowd churned.

"What about the workers? Surely the new, er, *addition* to their building was an issue?"

"You'd think. A few actually tried to go inside, but the doors didn't budge. So they joined their coworkers."

"And by joined, you mean?"

"What do you think? They all took a ride, pole in one hand, briefcase in the other."

BY THE NEXT morning it seemed that everyone was aware of our town's latest additions, and the streets hummed with an unusual frenzy. All through my walk I saw people peeking out from their windows, their doorways, rushing to and fro in various states of winter dress, many inspecting the strange growths from afar, many more throwing themselves at the things with rabid fervor. I told myself that I had left home early to drop off my library books before work, but I couldn't help but slow my pace to gawk as I passed each growth. It was safe to say that the developments were no longer isolated incidents, and on the short trip to the library alone (only a mile or so) I saw both a pop-gun shooting gallery which sprouted from the concave skull of a disused apothecary and a drop ride that burst out from the roof of a squat furniture store like the tip of a shining spear. After depositing my books, I waited to watch the monolith hoist a carriage to its tip only to let the people plummet. It didn't look very fun.

Work was slow, which was good considering that Antonio and I were the only employees who bothered to show up. Throughout our shift we must have served less than ten customers, and thus we spent most of our time in heated conversation. I told him about the tumorous carousel and how an unending stream of people had been riding it non-stop all day.

"Of course they have. Why wouldn't they? Our parks are landfills, our university is a tomb, our sports are a joke, and our arts are worse. Where do you—" He paused. "Well, maybe not you, but where would someone *sane* really want to spend their time, at a carnival or in a cafe?"

I snorted. "It's just a carousel. A carousel submerged in an office building. Not exactly someone sane's idea of a carnival."

"Maybe it was 'just a carousel' yesterday, but if you were to look again, you'd find something quite different. Haven't you noticed? They've been changing. The northwestern ridge's wound, so generously opened by the wheel, has festered. Now if you visit the site—although I know you won't—you'll find the land is swollen; it exudes all manner of strange scents. The whole district is tender now, pockmarked with unattended popcorn stands and cutout boards. Yes, I'm sure you'll see, the carnival is coming together."

By late afternoon, the morning's commotion had settled, and it seemed as if the township had now divided itself into two camps. The first were the denialists, those who still nestled snug in their lighted apartments or worked their dreary stations with myopic focus. The others were the resigned, whose ranks made up the densely packed queues which zipped across streets and down dark alleys, a sea of cold souls sporting the same, mask-like expression of subdued anticipation. I saw one group who shivered together before a newly born arcade, the flashing neon of its facade shading their faces and clothes with poisonous hues. My first feelings passing them were of revulsion, then pity, but by the time I reached the leaning district in which Mangrove Street was nestled, I began to form a strange admiration. Their embrace of the phenomena was honest and straightforward, and next to them, the denialists looked pathetic. After all, the denial of the rides did little more than ratify their existence: those nestled in their lighted apartments had drawn their shades, and the fools still at work prepared their stores for nonexistent customers.

Not that I was any better. The closer I drew to the former offices, the more it not only seemed natural, but necessary to construct an elaborate fantasy, one where despite Antonio's warning and all corroborating evidence, the complex's disease did not progress and had instead, if not reversed, then at least stalled. Perhaps now with the multitude of new and exciting growths throughout town, the interest in the carousel would have died out. Soon, without proper nourishment, it would wither and retreat.

The fantasy collapsed when I reached Mangrove Street. The virus had progressed, and the office complex was gone. It was as if the building had never been erected in the first place, leaving in its absence a square lot whose corners and edges were free of the expected imprints, rebar, or rubble. All there was, all it seemed there had ever been, was the carousel, a red-and-white rash softly oozing and sweetly smelling. A line trailed up to its bulk. Holsten's was closed—the calliope was louder than before.

As I fled home I discovered an unusual sentiment bubbling up in the back of my head. I mourned the office building, the anonymous structure which loomed outside Holsten's window night and day. I thought I would trade anything, anything at all, to return that horrible carousel for three stories of such comfortable grey: that warm, lovable temple of nothing.

YESTERDAY MORNING I WENT to work only to find it empty. The windows were darkened and there were no signs that the morning crew had even attempted entry. It seemed that most other workers acted equivalently, and thus the town had functionally ceased to operate as such. In the absence of a comfortable order, my fellow holders-on either gave in to the lure of the strange growths or otherwise acted without aim, wandering in a daze and staring at the developments, their faces showing a familiar cocktail of confusion, disgust, and awe. They reminded me of small pets, lost in new habitations. I went home.

Antonio was waiting outside my apartment. He grinned as I approached, and reaching into a black bag, withdrew a large bottle of scotch.

"Care for a chat?" he asked. "Dispatches from the front?"

I placed the bottle on my counter and poured two drinks. My apartment smelled sour and was crowded with books—I hadn't hosted in a while. Antonio sat in my reading chair, and I took the bed. Briefly he parted the curtains which had been drawn since

Autumn, and laughed.

"Have you seen the view?"

"No. How's the refinery keeping?"

"It's a water slide." He snorted. We shared a toast to its memory and drank.

"The mayor gave an address this morning," he said. "Not that anyone bothered to show."

"How was it?"

"Typical. He waddled out from town hall and weaseled about 'new developments' which are 'concerning and exciting' a 'small, but significant few.' Someone asked him if he was going to try and do anything to reverse, destroy, or contain the developments, and he just said his 'people' were 'looking into it.'" Antonio laced his quotations with sneers. "He said we should just sit and wait to see how 'developments unfold.' Developments! He doesn't know anything. What it's doing, what it wants, he doesn't even know what it is. Nobody does."

"And you do?" I asked.

He shrugged.

"I think it's a virus."

"What kind of virus infects buildings? What turns cities into carnivals?"

"I don't know. But at least I can tell you that." He took a gulp before adding, "And at least I'm not in charge."

Our conversation turned to the shape of the developments themselves, and Antonio was more than happy to share his latest findings. He told me of the most fantastical things: miniature trains that ran on webs of rail through crooked alleys of undesirable districts, blowing their whistles in the early hours of the morning; lengths of blackened sewers which had been converted into tunnels of love, neon-lit passages where the constant flow of sewage inexplicably gave way to rose-smelling waters on which bobbed white, dove-shaped gondolas; the errant tracks of unfinished roller coasters that spiraled off into heaven like the mutant spires of Gaudí. He spoke of them all with great reverence and a seemingly limitless joy; every adjective was accompanied by sparkles in his beady eyes. Each of my inquiries only seemed to prompt horrible new details, and I soon learned for my own sake not to prod further. The more I thought I grasped the phenomenon's reach, the less I wanted to know.

The day passed swiftly. The bottle emptied and he presented a flask, which in time emptied too. By nightfall we were properly trashed, and as our conversation turned to lighter fare, I made the mistake of assuming he had finished his apocalyptic report. I should've known he'd save the 'best' for last. It was just as he was making to leave that he stopped suddenly and said, with a drunken slur:

"Oh, one more thing. I forgot to tell you, something very important happened yesterday. Very important."

"Yes?"

"Yes—early yesterday morning, in a house not far from here, a mother awoke to the sound of rushing water. At first, she thought there was a storm, but through her window she could see it wasn't raining. So then she wondered if perhaps her building had a burst pipe, but that didn't make much sense either, because the water was incredibly loud and the sound suggested great force, as if her bed had been moved directly next to some cataract waterfall. So she got out of bed, slipped on her robe, and opened her bedroom door only to discover that it was more like the waterfall had been moved to her. Because right there, bisecting her second-story hall, was a metal chute funneling roaring rapids. She stared at it for a while, this metal chute which cut down through her roof and leveled out at the base of her kitchen below—her kitchen which, thanks to a large rectangle carved around the ceiling and floor surrounding the protrusion, was now clearly visible. Even though she had just ridden the Ferris wheel two days before, the mother didn't even remotely comprehend what she was seeing until a cylindrical carriage full of people shot down through her house, splashing her—and the already soaked hallway—with frigid water. It was then that she understood that her home was now the host of a log flume.

"Terrible, right? Just imagine it here, in your apartment—it would make your life unbearable. But it gets worse. See, unlike you, she had a child. And standing there, watching that log flume drop, she realized that very child, a boy no more than fifteen months old, was in his crib in the nursery across the hall. On the other side of the ride. Now, there was no way around that chasm, and her only chance was to jump it. A terrifying situation, to be sure, and her bravery is certainly to be applauded, because the moment the next carriage of dull-eyed strangers dipped past, she took off running and jumped the chasm. She made it across of course, and after taking a moment to collect herself, threw open the nursery door.

"But when she opened the door, she froze. The room had changed—the carpeted floors were patchy with plastic grass and the baby-blue walls had been repainted to resemble the horizon of some fantastic bayou, all mossy thickets and shadows and little round fireflies shining like stars. And she scanned this bedroom slowly as if to delay the inevitable, because when she came to her son's crib, she saw it was gone. In its place was a plastic tree stump, a thickly ringed pedestal on which sat a large badger of grotesque proportions. The badger sat on its hindquarters as a human would, with an oversized head, an oversized grin, and two oversized eyes; eyes that blinked with a rattling shutter-click, like a camera. It wore baggy corduroy overalls and a red-and-white bandanna was wrapped around its neck. It may have looked like a monster, but its motions revealed it to be just a humble animatronic, arms jerking sharply up and down, eyes darting to the left, then the right, before blinking and repeating the process, all in the span of a few seconds. The mother approached the thing, it whirred softly. She trembled, she touched its head, silicone fur stabbed her palm. She looked into its eyes and she knew. In no way did it resemble her child, but she just knew, beyond a doubt, that this creation had not replaced him—it *was* him.

"So she fell to her knees and wept. And the metal chimera—her former son—looked to the left, it looked to the right, it blinked its eyes, and it did so again. Today the whole house has been transformed. The animatronics—there are two now—are on full display, and their routine is rather delightful. I'm sure there will be more of their ilk soon." He hiccuped. "It's all very exciting."

THIS MORNING I FOUND that work had closed permanently—the old cafe was now the host of some shoddy dark ride, wherein carts weaved through what, based on the gothic exterior, I could only assume were a series of gauche horror shows. Freshly out of a job, I decided to play flaneur and went about further mapping the town's decay. By now the infection had consumed a solid third of the buildings, and it became easy enough for the eye to skip over the particulars, the packed-together rides merging into a single gaudy thicket, a bramble of lights and tracks and thunderous rumblings. I need not explain all of the grotesques I saw, although I will describe the one that finally stopped me in my tracks. It was the library. The windows had been removed, the walls were painted white (marked with a low band of blue shark-tooth waves), and a staircase climbed where the entrance once stood. The stout form was now used as the base for a pendulum ride, wherein a suspended pirate ship carriage swung above spurting jets of cerulean-dyed water. I watched it lurch, and for a moment wished I had just held onto those books for only a few days more.

It was late by the time I returned to my building, and after my journey it was no great surprise to find a zig-zagging queue assembled in front of the vestibule. A large motorized wheel had bisected the upper floors diagonally and hung like a crashed UFO. Grey-faced strangers whirled through the ghost of my apartment. Antonio sat besides the entrance, a nearly-emptied bottle in hand. He grinned.

"There you are! I was starting to worry this one had already eaten you up. Sorry about the sight—not the most glamorous amusement, I know. I don't mean to brag, but mine's got a top-spin. What's with the face? Come on, have a drink."

He shivered as he rose from the snow. I took the bottle and finished it.

"Thatta boy. Hope you liked it—good chance it's your last." He nodded to the queue assembled to our side. "I'm getting in line. Care to join me?"

"Not a chance. I'm leaving."

Antonio laughed, slapped my shoulder.

"Sure, sure—of course you are. Ever the dreamer, huh."

"I'm serious. I'm going, now."

"Ah, so you are …" A wistful smile crossed his face. "Not one for dignity in defeat. Well, okay then. It was nice knowing you, really. I think we had some fun."

We did. I nodded and left.

Night was dark and starless. Snowflakes drifted down gently upon flat roofs and crooked eaves. Everything was blanketed equally, and in the stillness of this winter midnight, a sort of equilibrium was achieved between the transforming buildings and those few still in chrysalis. It was the harmony that comes only through dilapidation, the perfection of ruins, of industrial plants reclaimed by vines or forgotten shrines half-submerged in swamp. The town's people were absent: were they sleeping, or had they already been absorbed? I suppose it didn't matter. Soon nothing here would matter. I'd be gone and the whole town could just be some bad dream, a ghost story I'd tell my perfectly ordinary peers in my new home of loving grey.

Yet still, as I trekked across town, I couldn't help but find the rides to be oddly amicable companions. The glow of their lighted facades carved a varicolored path through the streets, while the whirs of the machinery, still functioning sans riders, possessed a calming quality, akin to the rhythmic yawning of ocean waves. The further I went, the less I recognized, and despite it all I did not mind when the town slipped away and I found myself cutting through the wilderness, a teeming jungle of light, of color, of dull metal sheen and sharp metal clacking. I didn't mind the canopy of chain swings and hanging coasters, the pervasive miasma of buttered popcorn and frying oil, the beaming faces of animated beasts which waved from sculpted caves. Only occasionally would I find a patch of familiar street, and it wouldn't be until I spotted some barely intact landmark that I would realize that yes, the spotted tilt-a-whirl to my left was once a decrepit meat market, or indeed that the clanking hall of animatronic presidents was City Hall just yesterday. It would be a lie to say they weren't improvements.

It was early morning by the time I reached the station. I bought my ticket at a striped booth. When would the next train arrive? I didn't know, it didn't matter. My mission was all but accomplished. So I decided to wait facing the town. The buildings are sparse here, and only a single ride stands across from the platform. They're bumper cars, but more than that, they're floating leaves on a silver lake, drifting aimlessly on some hidden current. I've been watching for a while now, sitting on the bench, swaying in the cold. Somehow it's only just now occurred to me that I have never ridden bumper cars before. Nor carousels, nor roller coasters, and not one drop ride.

It's lonely on this platform. Something rumbles beneath the earth. The train should be here soon.

PERRY RUHLAND is a writer and filmmaker based in Chicago. His writing has previously been published in *Baffling Magazine*, *The Cafe Irreal*, *Vastarien Magazine*, *The Book of Queer Saints*, and *ergot.press*. A selection of his poetry and prose has been released as *Torture Gardens*.

THE LOW THING

Eli Wennstrom

Clouded by his cigarette smoke, Britt found the thought of entering the Pageant almost tolerable. He stood across the street from the stately venue. Tonight, alienating himself from it for as long as possible was essential to his survival. He was to remain an observer of the teeming crowd flushed by the cold, sending up smoke curtains through the crisp autumn air in a grasp at repose. Until the show began.

Here they all were, Britt included, to see a band formed long enough ago that this year it was old enough to drink. He exhaled another curtain to distract himself.

Night had arrived in St. Louis and, as the last stragglers were ushered into the Pageant, its predictable quilt of quiet fell contemplatively across the city. Cars slowed to a crawl in the street and blinked their eyes against the stiff wind and its leaves. A sweet burning smell appeared and evaporated with the draft. *A siren call*, Britt thought, *that I could follow to anywhere else*. After all, within half an hour the crowd would disperse from the merch table and the bar and clap in the dark for the band's arrival. Britt's Newport would be crushed into the ashtray beside him, and he would be forced to join them in concert. The carbonized food-smell on the street was something of a final temptation; he abated it with another menthol, then followed the flow of traffic.

BRITT'S GLASSES FOGGED as soon as he crossed the threshold into the lobby. He floated past the ticket scanners and merch setup, joining the sea of band tees and denim in the main hall. Stage light danced across the un-chipped paint of a stolid creamsicle Stratocaster, and Britt would consciously avoid meeting its expectant gaze for the next five minutes. He wished he was drunk.

A bartender stood surprisingly patient for the several moments it took Britt's mind to catch up with where his body had led. "A Sidecar," he said quickly.

The server looked back blankly. "We don't have that. What kind of beer is it? City Wide's good if you want something kind of hoppy."

"It's a cocktail," Britt said. "It was the first thing that came to mind; don't know why. I'm not sure I've ever even had one. I'll take an Old Fashioned." He ran the fingers of his right hand through his beard and exhaled hotly into his palm.

Behind closed eyes, Britt imagined a cardboard box (its size was indeterminate and irrelevant). Near the box was a mass of black viscera, pulsating and oozing across the floor of his mind. It collected easily, and in one practiced movement, it was inside that box with the top folded in overhead. With the sound of a second layer of tape tearing, Britt returned to the bar.

"—saying I'm not sure what to expect," another man at the bar repeated over the music. "For some reason, I thought Mark might finally bring the original lineup back for this. Would've been nice."

"Yeah, I wouldn't have minded that. I'm sure they're busy with other things; didn't have the time to tour. Kids, maybe? He's the draw, anyway, y'know?"

"Yeah, just think it would've been nice for—"

"I'm sorry, sir, I didn't ask which whiskey you wanted with that," the bartender said, tapping a laminated cheat sheet on the countertop.

"Something local, please." The bartender nodded and turned back to the liquor lineup. Britt returned his attention to the buzz about the bar, but the conversation he'd honed in on had ended. One of the men paid and Britt watched the pair filter through the crowd toward the front of the standing section. A glint of orange caught his eye. He snapped his gaze back to the bar. "Thanks, I'll keep it open," he said with the exchange of his debit card.

Pushing the peel aside, Britt took a pull from his drink. The house lights began to fade.

TWO HOURS LATER, the dregs of the concert lingered by the tour bus out back of the venue. Their heads were on a swivel; these were not the audience members who had carefully maintained their cool, disinterested personas during the concert and departed early. This group spoke drunkenly among one another, poster tubes tapping at their shoulders, reminiscing about the evening, or recounting their shared musical history. Were it not for the obfuscation of the night, the perpetual pall of smoke in front of his face, and the pair of glasses he had picked up since, some may have recognized the band's founding bassist, standing a considered distance from the stage door.

"You know," Mark's voice came from behind, "I honestly thought you'd flaked, man." Britt turned to meet his former frontman's grin, still holding fort against his iconic forest of whiskers. That beard wore several stripes of grey, now. Over the first few minutes of their reunion, Britt couldn't shake the sensation of rediscovering his own age in the medicine cabinet mirror. Between words of warm reception, Mark threw a few keen glances at the throng. Over the course of their conversation, he shifted several times to avoid notice. The self-possession that Britt had seen develop in Mark during their youth had crystallized in the intervening years. Next to it, however, nested a nervousness taken shelter behind his eyes.

"Good show, Mark. You still sound like the same guy. Those kids are good."

"The new band?" Mark asked, placing a hand on Britt's shoulder. He let out a peal of high, percussive laughter before lowering his profile once again. "They *are* pretty good, right? Kids . . . they're older than my kid, but you're not wrong. Jason's doing right by you every stop on the tour."

"Bass."

Mark nodded, then gestured broadly toward the fans crowding the tour bus. "They go crazy for your little breakdown in *Outlast Me* every night—you saw. Jason nailed that one in the audition, even. He said that record was the first CD he ever bought."

"That makes my knees hurt," Britt exhaled as he put his cigarette out against the brick wall. "I think he played it better than me. Better than I could now, definitely."

"He plays it technically and he loves it."

"Well, I hope he does. Want one?"

"No, I gave it up. I decided I didn't want my, ah, *vessel* to be a slave to some product anymore. Or my temple, or my etcetera." His beard shifted around a wry smile. "Kidding."

"Right," said Britt feeling his jacket pockets for his lighter.

"Actually, hold that cig. Are you parked around here?"

"Just across the way."

"I haven't been home in . . . I'm not sure how long. Since Dad died, I haven't been out to visit, and our usual tours never bring us out this way. Ticket sales just don't reward it."

"Had to stop for the nostalgia circuit, though."

"Sure, it's an anniversary tour. You have to take things back where they started."

The wind picked up, and both men pulled their unzipped jackets shut against their chests in perfect time with one another. It was late enough in Fall that the breeze had begun growing out of her old clothes. Her thin, sharp limbs—scythe-like—cut into bystanders after dark, forecasting the coming season. The two old men stood rigid as she whipped through their thin corpora and off into the starless sky.

"Was the weather always this miserable?" asked Mark as he hazarded a stretch to pull his socks up further.

"I like it," Britt replied between gritted teeth.

"I'm imagining a slight change of scenery. How's a 'nostalgia tour' around the Lou sound? We can hit some old haunts, get a few too many drinks along the way."

"Yeah. No visiting with your adoring mob?" Britt nodded back toward the tour bus.

"Ah, the other guys will come out."

"I think I recognize a few of them from our bar days. I don't think they want to meet anyone you hired within the year."

Mark laughed, tighter than before. "Ouch. Maybe you want to go over there. I bet they'd be into meeting you more than any of the new ones."

Britt paused. "No, I don't think so."

"I see them every night; let's get out of here."

On their amble back to the car, neither man spoke. Leaves caught underfoot crunched. Any conversation would overtake them, and even Mark's reflexive witticism was exceeded by his desire to listen to them instead. Another harsh wind blew across Delmar Boulevard, spiriting away the lights inside the Pageant. By the time Britt had opened his car door, the tour bus assembly had fallen silent. Their silhouettes trembled in the gloom.

AUTUMN AIR BLUSTERED in through the passenger-side window, and Britt's flushed face leaned out to welcome it. Now, four Old Fashioneds and several hours into early morning, the wind's roar didn't bother him. If he could dial in on the sound, it might even distract from the fact that his head was rolling between his shoulders of its own volition.

Mark had more than held his own at the hole-in-the-wall finds the two had stopped at tonight, and he had generously covered each tab. Every successive bar was lit dimmer than the last, and warmer. By the ultimate stop (that he could remember), Britt was touching his sweating glass to his ears to cool them. Mark's voice had seemed to reverberate from the taproom's cold stone walls, filling the space with the dissonant ghosts of his adulthood successes and failures. His table partner's reticence was not an obstruction, but a podium from which to share increasingly intimate details. Decades of stories came together in Britt's mind to form an image not unlike one of the crumbling brick houses that dotted his home city. He could understand the general shape of his oldest friend's life, but there was spalling across time and within the stories themselves. *What are the odds*, he'd wondered, *that a man could emerge completely clean from every story of his life?* Britt wasn't sure how long Mark had been driving his car.

"Do you remember the night we came up with *Daphne*?" Mark asked, piercing the night's first prolonged silence. He leaned into the steering wheel, squinting through the windshield. Britt murmured an affirmation. "You were going to just throw out that little riff that we built it on. It's funny how that—"

"Not throw it out. It was a drill. A warm-up."

"You were just playing it without saying anything, man." Mark laughed. "If I hadn't craned my twenty-year-old neck around . . . I practically *forced* you to keep playing it. We would've never made the best song on that first album. Our hit!" He shook his head. "Would never have made our first hit."

"It wasn't supposed to be a song, just a drill," Britt replied. He straightened up in his seat and slowly became conscious of just how hard his heart was beating in his chest. The distance between each of Mark's syllables was smoothed over by alcohol.

"But it *is* more than that. That bassline is a part of something. If you're in a store, pick up a guitar and play that part, I can guarantee that someone else will hum the melody or bang out the drums from the recording on their thighs. What you wrote doesn't exist in an amp in your bedroom." Mark paused, searching. The rehearsed words swirled around one another in a quagmire. He settled on: "I made it bigger. Or, actually, subsumed it into a bigger thing. That's why I'm the leader, Britt. I guess." He swallowed. "I know a good sound when I hear it." He shrugged and looked at Britt with eyes milky in the windshield moonlight. There was no recognition there.

It seemed to Britt that all of a sudden, the car was going very fast down this country road. He was floating above the ground, careening through the pitch the car was submerged in. Terror's fingers laced between his ribs and prodded his insides. *Where are we?* There were no lights lining the street, and through the headlights, Britt could only see some low brush twisting in the wind. A railroad ran to their right. "What road is this?"

"We're just . . . tooling," Mark replied. "We're north."

"Are we in Illinois?"

He didn't reply, focused singularly on piloting the car down a steep hill. Britt's breath seized in his throat, and his eyes widened instinctually against their heavy lids. "I don't think you were out that long," Mark said. The car rattled as it reached the hill's base and skittered back to level with the road.

"You shouldn't be driving," Britt mumbled, pulling himself upright. "Stop the car."

"I've got us."

"That's what I'm . . . " Britt struggled to bring his thoughts together. "Pull over." Mark inhaled sharply through his nose, showing no signs of breaking. "Mark, this is my car. Caroline is expecting me back tonight and we're not even going the right way."

"I said I've got us, man," Mark started, blood rushing to his face and the gas pedal at once.

"Mark, neither of us should be sitting in that seat. Pull us over and I'll call someone to come get us." There was no response, save the hammering in his own head. "This is my car—"

"I heard you. No one's coming out here, it's the middle of the night. We're just taking a drive . . . I'll get you home. We used to do this all the time."

The car drifted about the road, which ran headlong into darkness only feet ahead. Britt attempted several measured breaths, succeeding only in panicking himself with the belabored breathing that his sober mind could have attributed to drink. Any remaining hope of meditation was dashed by the rattling of his car over the pockmarked byway. When he shut his eyes, the world pitched around him. He kept them open.

The resentment, immemorial, didn't bubble or rise but struck repeatedly against Britt's skull like a rock beaten on pavement. It may have arrived years earlier had they reunited at a mutual's funeral (Mark's routine was to send flowers in his place), but instead, it careened through Britt's maudlin blood and threatened to exit his mouth as a scream. Drinking, it seems, slows all functions except the feverish ones; those took twice as much effort to hold down deep, now. He poked his face out the window in case anything was to escape between breaths. *It's only one night*, he negotiated with himself, *and it's almost over*. Alongside the car, there was movement along the base of a hill. A gasp.

The car bucked. Britt was propelled backward, landing partially on the gear shift and emergency brake. Mark yelped unintelligibly, jerking the steering wheel, and audibly colliding with various elements of the interior. Tires wailing, the guide rail sank screaming into the passenger-side tail, warping the metal around the wound. The air in his lungs escaped in one rasped puff as Britt jerked forward into the car door. The road collapsed into stillness.

Britt shifted back fully into his seat, cataloging a lateral cut across his forearm, what he assumed to be a bruised rib, and his aching teeth. He ran his fingers along the cut and winced; not in pain, but at the discovery of blood streaked along a protrusion from the railing. His glasses, retrieved from the footwell, sat unevenly below his brow; this discovery, surprisingly, was the most affecting of the crash.

"What were you doing?" Mark murmured as he looked across the road. His door flew open, and he erupted half-stumbling, half-spilling out of it and into the street. With the passenger door flush against the guide rail, Britt followed, fumbling over the center console. Mark cried out gutturally, then, composing himself: "Stop!"

Looking up from his awkward position in the car, Britt saw the subject of Mark's demands: the man fled without reserve into a thicket lining the opposite side of the asphalt. He appeared to be balding, possibly bearded, and dressed in a heavy flannel shirt—that was all Britt could recover through the slivers between trees; November mist masked him entirely within seconds.

"You saw him?" Mark said, pivoting back to the car. "Did you get a good look?" Britt shook his head. "Ah, Christ." Mark made to pace but only limped a distance and crouched down on the road. Britt aligned himself in the driver's seat, collecting his memories leading up to the accident. He felt cold for the first time in hours, and the thick beads of mist collecting on his cheeks ran races down his shirt collar. His hand trembled violently as he produced the phone from his pocket. "God, *God*," Mark began again. "My leg. I try to do the responsible thing . . . "

"What's wrong with your leg?" No response. "My calls won't complete here, what provider do you have?"

Mark pushed himself up to stand. "Why would you let me drive?

If you thought that I shouldn't—and you *know* I don't know these roads like I used to—why the hell would you give me the keys, Britt?" He thrust them outward as he said it, vigorously rattling them.

"I don't remember giving them to you."

"You put these keys in my hand."

The resentment was back in his throat, but so bewildering was the flood of anxiety, fury, and pain that it was rendered speechless. "That's . . ." he began. *Playing the victim, just like when he fired the rest of us.* "That's really low. How can you put this on me, Mark? Give the deflection a rest for once." *Building a career off my work, the songs every night about being "taken advantage of" by girls half his age, crashing my . . .* "If you can, hold it until we call triple-A," the discontent said, unable to resist a turn of the screw before being restrained again. Mark stood very still in the road.

Breathing in the heavy air, and suddenly hot-faced once again, Britt exited the car and stretched. No headlights had shone at either end of the road since the accident. In fact, it struck Britt for the first time that there was no other vehicle parked in the vicinity; none for the man who caused the accident to have emerged from. *The real cause of the crash is twenty feet away nursing his leg.* The man had run from the right side of the road.

Surveying the immediate vicinity of his car, there was nothing obviously amiss. Past the guide rail, brush and short trees rustled in the breeze; just beyond them, a hill's silhouette maintained. The car was immobilized. Britt slunk about the crime scene, documenting: the piercing that killed it, the rear wheel bent outward unnaturally (certainly a broken axle), and the red taillight spatter that glittered beneath his phone's flash. He swiped back through those photographs in review, pausing on the first he'd taken. In it, past the car glistening with dew, the contours of the hill were brought into sharp relief by an orange glow behind it. Looking up, the light was even more glorious to the naked eye. He wasn't sure how it had gone unnoticed; the dark landscape below gave Britt the impression of looking up at an anvil, mantled with some hot ore. There was sound in that direction, too.

The hillside was easily navigated. Once he was over the railing, Britt's work boots were able to find footholds without a search; at this time of night, he couldn't see where to step, regardless. The glow shared more of itself the closer he stepped: under the soft rain patter, there was a dog baying, metal moving on metal, and fabric flapping in the wind. More players in the strange symphony became clear with each stride. It was not until Britt approached the crest that it occurred to him to check in with his former bandmate. Turning back, he was unsettled to discover they were sharing a plane on the hillside.

"I didn't hear you over there. Leg better?" Britt asked, attempting to soften his tone.

"I didn't see you at first, either," Mark said, staring at the light. "Sounds like there might be someone who can give us a hand." Without another word, both men returned to their trek.

It was only a short distance to the hilltop, where they stopped to look down at the glow's face. Workmen bustled, breaking down tents, folding and dissembling attractions, and packing trucks and their hitched trailers full of equipment. Floodlights, appropriately, flooded the valley and sky. She was a carnival, though this wasn't an ideal place for her. From his vantage, Britt could only see one road running through the center of the grassy lot, and the illuminated surroundings were marked with gullies, making for difficult parking. He guessed that the country road would connect on the far side of the hill with the one where his car's corpse lay now.

The descent was easier, as it usually is. Matching step for step, Mark kept pace with Britt all the way to the outskirts of the amusement park. Several large, pinstriped tents were still standing in this portion of the carnival, but no workers were in sight. Mark's limp suddenly returned, so he took a seat on a worn wooden bench and ran his fingers persistently over the keys in his pocket, searching for nothing. Britt followed his partner's lead and gave himself an allowance to recover. It was late, after all. A few minutes wouldn't save the car or get him in bed at a reasonable hour.

Finally coming to rest on the fairgrounds, his injuries faded back into focus. From somewhere deep, the soreness emerged and spread back across the places marked by the wreck. It moved like the warmth from a campfire, he thought, only inverted.

Several minutes on, a younger man emerged from between two tents walking a Boston Terrier mix. The drizzle didn't seem to bother either of them. Britt waved him down casually, downplaying his emergency for reasons unknown to even himself. "You two look worse for wear," the man said.

"We had a minor accident on the road across the way. On the other side of the hill, I mean. Can we use your phone?"

"That was you? Fifteen, twenty minutes ago?" Britt nodded, though the timeframe struck him as at once too recent and too removed. "That sounded gnarly. I don't have my phone on me, I'll have to go get it from my trailer, at the other end of the grounds. You stay put; it probably isn't healthy for you to be moving around right now. I'll make the call for an ambulance and come right back."

"Thank you. What's her name?"

"June," he said, stooping to scratch between her ears. Britt approached and did the same. The dog's head grooved side to side under his hand. "You should see her in the show, she rides a horse. No kidding. Doesn't even need a saddle. I've got a video I can share once I'm back." He walked on, June tagging closely behind.

"This is absurd," Mark said listlessly. Britt agreed. Mark brought himself to his feet and took a long look at the contents of this end of the carnival, soon taking to inspecting their surroundings up close.

Britt assumed his seat on the bench, gingerly feeling out the bruising on his right abdomen.

"Fortune teller," Mark sighed, pulling back the flap of a tent in purple and blue. He moved on to its neighbor. "Oh, a little dirt rink. Maybe for dogs and horses." Between tents, Jack-o-lanterns melted into the straw and dirt ground and were obviously unhappy about it. Mark took care to leave them be. He opened the last tent, orange and red, and paused. He flashed the light of his cell phone inside. "Mirror maze," he said. He stepped aside to look further in, allowing Britt to make out the epigraph himself:

HALL OF MIRRORS
MEET YOUR TRUE SELF

"You should go in," Britt said.

"Maybe the accident broke something important," Mark snapped.

"You're right, that's just something you'd write a song about doing."

"What does *that* mean?"

"Afraid of what you'd see?" Britt gestured toward the Hall.

Scowling, Mark turned his back. In a blink, he was shouldering the tent flap and striding into the unlit maze, Britt's keys jangling in his jacket pocket. Britt wasn't far behind.

Stopping to draw his phone, Britt noticed an additional line on the attraction's sign, beneath the announcement he'd seen before. In a slightly smaller (yet severe) script, it read:

ENTER ONE AT A TIME (ENFORCED)

He stepped past a derelict stool dusted with ticket stubs, wiped his glasses on his shirt, and entered.

WHEN APPROACHING A DEAD END, the phone's flashlight bounced into infinity in every direction. It was something of a relief. Occasionally the maze would cease curling in on itself and provide Britt with a surprisingly long hallway, the end of which was so tenebrous that the light didn't penetrate. A dead end might delay one an extra few seconds from arriving at the exit, but crossing the length of a hallway was so disquieting that it inspired him to turn back.

The men didn't speak to one another, though Britt could hear the tap of footsteps somewhere ahead of him. It was bracingly quiet otherwise. The number of walls and the thick canvas of the tent effectively insulated the Hall from all outside sound. The further inside Britt trod, the crisper the air felt. Consequently, the heat of his own body quickly became nigh impossible for him to ignore. His belly was a woodstove within the first five minutes inside, while the environment grew indifferently colder and thinner.

When it became obvious that Mark was moving too steadily ahead for the two to meet, Britt directed his focus away from his own discomfort and toward the subtle differences in the glass that comprised the maze. Many panes were scuffed or scraped in their own unique places; one, in particular, had become a place for couples to enshrine their initials. Their signatures and hearts petered out in the last foot from the ceiling, though a handful were unusually high up. There were trick mirrors every so often; the kind to spread you thin or thick, but the effect was mostly lost in the phone's sterile glare.

There were no decorative markings or molding crowning the mirrors, they simply stood straight. Straight and solid, reaching all the way up to a mirrored ceiling. Lightbulbs hung cold along their edges.

Britt adhered to the path of the right wall, not removing his hand from it for a moment. It was a trick he had learned from his father at a local farm's corn maze; not useful for 30 years, but also not lost along the way. If the trace remained unbroken, he would eventually emerge. Rounding a sharp right corner, he encountered another straight ahead. Just as he took his first step into it, he heard loud, trembling breaths and shuffling in the shadows ahead.

"Was that you? Britt?" Mark's voice came from the distance.

"I'm down here," Britt replied. There was a long pause in conversation, and the sounds of movement filled it.

"Somebody touched me."

"Come back this way, let's get out of here." Britt stood rigidly at his end of the hall. Then, comforting himself: "It was just someone trying to pack this thing up."

"No, this guy was grabbing at me."

Turn around and leave. Britt crept toward the dark and Mark's unusually genuine tone. "It's all right, Mark," he began, strangling the tremble out of his voice. "Not to sound too patronizing, but you're just drunk." Each touch of his hand to the chill glass was a cool relief; Britt was boiling in his shirt and light jacket, and his ribs throbbed. The truth was, in spite of the sickness coming on, he felt soberer now than he had since waking up that morning, and Mark's voice reflected the same. It was time to leave.

Ten feet deep, a sudden two-pane-wide opening in the mirrors appeared on the left, forking the path in two. "Left, or straight?" Britt called out. *He's in no hurry to leave, just abandon the car keys.* "Did you turn left or keep straight?" He looked down the remainder of the tunnel, waiting for any response. Something moved in his periphery, down the path through the left wall. In one slow, unbroken revolution, Britt's neck craned to gaze into the opening.

He saw a man, down the left passageway, returning his gaze. The figure was taller than Mark, and only visible as a fuzzy grey outline against the black path beyond him. The figure was obscured enough that it could have been something other than a man, but Britt could perceive, somehow, that it wasn't. Taking a trepidatious step forward, then another, Britt approached the passage; the voyeur remained hunched in his place. Britt opened his mouth, hoping for it to fill with questions or accusations. There was a bright light bobbing somewhere in the tunnel between the two men, growing with his advance toward the voyeur. It wasn't until his hand contacted the mirror in front of him that Britt recognized the light of his own phone. His own reflection stared back behind two lenses grey as silver dollars with fog. Britt snatched the glasses off his face and swiped his hand across them; replacing them, he swore that he saw the man slink around the corner ahead. The corner that existed within a mirror. Britt tapped on the glass in front of him, his reflection simulating the same motion.

Mark screamed somewhere down the long hallway. The mirror man had discovered him. *Leave.* It would be easier. *He deserves a scare.* But this was more than that. Britt snapped back down the hall, his legs moving quickly and uncertain under him, his light source flickering across dozens of surfaces and proving not much help. He burned beneath his damp clothes, but the momentum of his shoes carried him onward. The rubber soles stamping against the floor shook the glass on all surfaces, filling the aloof Hall with its insides' awful quavering. He connected with a dead end, then another, in his haste abandoning his father's heirloom method. Mark screamed again, and plead, and his collisions with the mirrored walls in the distance dispatched shockwaves to cancel out Britt's own. *Bang.* Britt cleared another corner. *Bang.* Another long hallway ahead, which he sprinted through with abandon. *Rattle.* Another turn, another curve into a dead end. The relentless barrage relented.

Britt's breathing filled the vacuum. He carried on through too many twists for a tent this size to contain. Out of the dark, a dripping shape lunged forth and wordlessly fled down the path Britt had just tramped. "Mark?" Hauling the energy together once more, Britt pursued Mark through the maze, catching flashes of his jacket past corner after corner. Landing at a dead end, the thought occurred to him: was the mirror man following? He pushed his body even harder, fleeing and chasing in equal measure. It was then that his phone blacked out.

Pitched into total darkness, panic set in in earnest. Britt waved his arms in wide arcs, striking nothing. The sound of uneven foot-fall reached past the blood pounding in his ears, towing him forward. Slower, now, though the steps ahead sounded more labored than before; he matched Mark's gait and carried on. There were footsteps behind him, too, Britt became certain of that. He stepped deliberately after Mark, hoping that their pursuer would lose pace and get caught in a false path. Later, he considered that the follower might have been trying to convince Britt to turn back and shadow its footsteps instead.

Humidity returned to the air, but it wasn't until the men neared the exit that Britt realized just how much the atmosphere had changed. He moved easier, slipping ever further from the oppressive emptiness. In a sudden, swift motion, floodlight breached the threshold of the Hall; Mark ducked under the tent opening and hobbled into its acceptance. The tent slipped shut once more, but in three long strides, Britt slammed it out of the way and collapsed into the early morning. For a moment, he simply embraced the ground. The cool, wet grass was uneven and coarse between his fingers; it was welcome.

The sound of collapse pried Britt from his homecoming. Mark, caught on a bit of fence, had crashed onto the base of the hill. Britt approached to pry him free. "*No*," Mark said firmly, whipping back to confront his former bandmate. Britt got his first look at Mark's new visage, then. Round and flowing with gore, his face was lit grotesquely by the harsh floodlight, and many of his features were so deeply cast in the contrasting shadows that they disappeared completely. Mark was a cubist interpretation of himself: parts of a nose, a puffed lower lip, straight lines of cheek, and two crooked, glinting eyes comprised the man. He raised a quivering hand, miming pushing Britt away; he obliged.

The last time Britt saw Mark Howe, he was scrambling over the hilltop they'd conquered together. He was rubbing the blood out of his face with his loose coat fluttering about in the wind. The early morning sky was grey with clouds.

Britt rode silently with the tow truck operator back into town. The car was totaled. A week later, the final leg of the tour was officially announced as canceled after three performances were postponed in a row. For as much of his life that had been trammeled by hypotheticals and plastered-over indignation, after the concert at the Pageant, Britt no longer found himself ruminating on that history. Otherwise, all that the night amounted to was an occasional unintelligible voicemail.

ELI WENNSTROM is a St. Louis-based author of strange happenings. Raised on Southern Gothic stories in Texas, he embraced the Weird once he relocated to his home in the Midwest. His work can be found in *Lovecraftiana* and *Ghostwatch Zine*; he can be found at his desk.

SOMEWHERE WARM ON A GOLDEN BEACH

Kevin Brown

5:45 A.M.

Skylar Mosely gunned the throttle on his old man's fishing boat and the nose lifted high off the dark water, the current splitting white around the aluminum body. Squinting, he snaked around the bends of the river, watching the dark treetops limned ahead. His earlobes were red and stinging. His eyes watered in the cold push of air.

An hour ago, he'd snuck out dressed in layers of hunting clothes and hitched the boat to the pick-up. It was his dad's truck and boat, and Skylar wasn't allowed to take them out alone. But he'd decided to after his dad came home tanked and smelling not like his mom's perfume. They'd yelled and cried and slammed things until he passed out, and she went to the Motor Inn Motel. This had been happening more and more, and Skylar figured that if they could have their places to go, so could he.

Skylar watched the snow-splotched banks slide by. Felt the foamy spray of water on the backs of his hands like ice needles. He bit down hard, and his jaw squared off and popped. He was sick of the liquor and women, the fighting and cruelty. Lately, he wondered what was going on in his old man's mind when he slammed tools in the garage. When he stabbed food on his plate as if it were alive, shoveling it in his mouth faster than he could chew and swallow. Always looking down or to the side, answering questions in grunts or nods. He wondered where that anger had come from and how far it was going to go.

Skylar eased off the throttle and angled the boat toward a fallen cedar near the bank. His dad had never taken him upriver this far and the land felt foreign and undiscovered. He'd heard game ran wild in this area because few people hunted it—if you were lucky enough to bag a good sized deer, getting it back would be a chore, and most folks didn't bother. But he figured he'd cross that bridge when and if he came to it.

He'd also heard stories of these woods being haunted. It was where that family, the Otis', had supposedly lived. Where, if you believed the tales, they were murdered—burned alive, one at a time. Son and daughter first. And according to the older folks in town, where the house stands to this day, the four charred spots were still burned into the floorboards.

Skylar stepped onto the muddy bank bottom and tied the boat off. Shouldered his .30-06 and looked around, his breath ghosting out white. Currents rolled and flecked in the river, but everything else was a numb silence. He climbed the bank by the jutting tree roots and stepped into the woods, sinking calf-high in the snow. He felt oddly comfortable, as if the land was closing its arms around him. Pulling him in a hug to its breast.

6:40 A.M.

Nature began to form and take shape with the light, the world one large Polaroid being shaken until it developed. The brush came alive, rattling. Twigs snapped. Parts of dead trees cracked off and popped the snow. It seemed the lighter it got, the louder. And colder.

Skylar sat on a dark tree root crooked out of the snow like a burned elbow. The wind seemed to come from all directions, chipping away at his face and neck. A few feathering snowflakes had turned into a sideways flurry, and it was hard to see more than thirty yards out. The snow's surface was smooth as white cake icing.

He flipped his collar up and slid his hands under his armpits, balancing the rifle in his lap. He imagined his mom shifting and tossing under worn motel sheets. Her face clenched in the middle, eyes red and raw. And his dad, still sprawled sideways on the bed, half-dressed and snoring. He couldn't understand why his father continued to stray off the straight, simple road he and Skylar's mom had been on for twenty-one years. Why he took highways and side roads headed in every direction but home.

He thought about their vacation a year ago. It was the last great time he could remember them having together. They'd gone to Clearwater, Florida, and every day they ate at a different seafood restaurant. He and his dad played Frisbee on the beach. Tossed hunks of bread in the air for the screeching seagulls to dive and catch, and watched the sun deflate into the horizon, where it watered off and on to somewhere, anywhere. In beach chairs behind him, his mom and dad sipped margaritas and laughed and kissed, while Skylar sat in the surf, curling his toes in the warm wet sand. The water foaming in and over and around him, then sliding metallic back into the sea.

He shifted on the root, looked out ahead, and thought about that old house. If it was really out here somewhere, all decayed and folding in on itself. Animal tracks and wads of shit everywhere. He wondered what direction it was supposed to be in. If he was close.

The way he'd heard it, the Otis' lived back here in the thirties. People called them river rats because they lived on what they took from the river. Some claimed to have seen them occasionally, running trotlines and barrel nets for fish and turtles. They were supposed to be inbred and ravaged by syphilis. Disfigured by chancres and patchy hair, pegged and notched screwdriver teeth. Brain disorders.

Story goes, they took in a couple of guys lost in the woods one night. What they didn't know was these guys had robbed and killed a goods store owner twenty miles north and took to the woods. They fed them, gave them a change of clothes, and beds for the night.

And sometime the next morning . . .

Skylar looked around, scanning the thickets and bottoms. He wondered if years ago, killers had actually come through this exact area, maybe rested on this same elbow root. If they saw chimney smoke mouse-tailing above the trees. Faint candlelight in the windows like eyes. He wondered if all those years ago, you could smell burnt flesh in the air. Blood and charred hair in the leaves. He figured not, because he'd also heard the Otis' weren't fried like witches, that they'd just moved on, farther upriver where the fish were more abundant. Lived and died the way most people lived and died. Uneventfully.

Some swear they never even existed.

To his left, there was a loud crack in the underbrush and he jerked around. Leaned forward and raised his rifle. Another snap and he saw it—a Jackrabbit working its nose in the air, ears twitching. It spun and sputtered into the tangle, and Skylar eased his gun back across his lap. Wiped his nose with the back of his hand. He glanced to his right and nearly fell backward, off the root.

Standing there, forty yards out and staring at him, was a large, wide-racked buck.

It had never made a sound. Just appeared out of nowhere like a ghost.

6:45 A.M.

Skylar whipped his gun up as the buck turned to bolt. He squinted, threaded the bead on its shoulder, and fired.

6:46 A.M.

Blood was everywhere. Standing where the deer had been, breathing heavy, he could still hear it bouncing through the thicket ahead. He wasn't sure where he hit him, but it was deep enough. Thick ropes of blood trailed off from where he stood, toward the sounds the deer was making.

Skylar ate a handful of snow, pinched his collar, and fanned his shirt. He looked back in the direction he'd come from, toward the river. Large foot divots in the snow like candle holes in cake frosting.

He turned back toward the unseen world snapping and popping and dying ahead. He started after it.

8:15 A.M.

Skylar leaned over, hands on his knees, trying to catch his breath. His lungs felt scrubbed raw inside and he coughed and spat. He'd come a ways, the deep snow hampering his movements. Several times he thought he'd lost the trail and was about to turn back, when a slash of red on a tree or a glob in the snow pulled him along. He'd been through a rotten cane patch woven with vines of briers, and farther, until looking back, the black oaks and cedar trees looked like walls. Like jaws closing out the open world forever.

Still coughing, Skylar yelled, "Better be one big fucking deer!" and his voice sounded small.

He kept going—up the incline of a ridge, along its spine. Down the slope, the snow sliding around him, and—

Before he heard it, he almost ran right into it. He dropped to his knees, slipped his coat off, and clutched a tree trunk. Leaning forward, he drank handfuls of icy stream water that swirled by, dark as the trees, then disappeared around the bend.

8:23 A.M.

Skylar wiped his mouth on his shirtsleeve and looked around. The trail picked up on the other side of the stream, and unless there was a narrower spot to cross, that was it. Curtain call. He was done.

He leaned back down for another drink, and the small bank loosened and caved. He whimpered and slipped face forward toward the water. Never breaking grip with the tree, his body spun and his legs went in instead.

He sunk gut deep, his feet hitting the bottom.

As quickly as he went in, he grabbed the tree with his other hand and pulled himself out. The water had taken his breath, and his clothes were slick and shiny and clinging to his body as if they were melting.

AN HOUR LATER.

Skylar's hands fluttered. His jaw quivered. He'd started back, following his own ghost of a trail, as the older tracks were disappearing, erased by the storm. He'd slid his coat on and jammed his hands under his armpits, carrying the rifle in his folded arms. But the shaking had intensified. His toes seemed to have disappeared a while back, and his pants were stiffening and freezing to his legs. He fell several times, and with each fall he left a little more of his energy, of himself, in the snow.

He reached the cane patch and made his way in. He scanned the ground, the tracks barely imprints on the surface. He went left, lost the trail. Turned back and followed the tracks he'd just made. The briers bit into his clothes, tore at his cheeks and ears. Cane sprung at his face, popping him in the forehead. He stumbled and regained balance. Turned and went in any direction, clawing, trying to find some landmark that looked familiar. "Please," he said, and saw an opening ahead. He went toward it in a rush, the thorns ripping into him, and finally made it out of the tangle. He stopped. Dropped to his knees.

There was the stream, the bank caved in by the tree.

He looked around. Every thicket and stunted cedar, log and bush looked the same. Black and white Xeroxed copies in all directions. He tried to stand and dropped his rifle. Tripped and sunk. He slammed his fist into the ice and screamed, but it muffled in the flurry. The wind moaned around him. For some reason, he pictured his mom on the nights she waited up for his dad, her eyes rimmed in tears. Imagined the *tack, tack, tacking* of her wedding ring on the tabletop.

And for the first time, he began to think he might die. Started to wonder if his death would somehow reunite his parents. Maybe make them see what real unhappiness is. Through his tragedy, their marriage would live on. A sacrifice of him for the better them.

He smiled and began to cry.

LATER.

Skylar nestled between two oak logs, draped his coat over his legs, and closed his eyes. His hands trembled in a violent blur and his lips had gone the color of veins under the skin. His eyelids bruise-purple and as translucent as a baby bird's. He tried to listen for a passing boat. Some sign that would show him the direction the river was in. Back to where his dad's boat was roped off and waiting to take him somewhere warm. To his family. His home. He was about to nod off when he heard a child's voice giggle and say, "You dead?"

He opened his eyes.

In front of him, a little girl was wrapped in a dirty brown coat, wearing yellow socks as mittens.

He started to cry again.

"You *ain't* dead!" she said. Tears slid off his cheeks and he shook his head "no."

She reached out and wrapped both hands around one of his, grunted, and tugged. He winced, snakes of pain coiling through his legs. She tugged harder and said, "Come *on*, silly." He shifted, and the cold around his joints seemed to crack and release. He staggered to his feet, a lapful of snow dusting down.

She turned to go, still holding one of his hands, but he didn't move. "Well?" she said. "You coming or ain't ya?"

He took a step and fell. She helped him up and he took another, then another, his movements jerky and stilted. He stared at the back of her head, her dirty blonde curls floating in the wind. In a breathless fragment, he said, "Where . . . we going?"

Not looking back, she giggled.

"Hey," he said, "do you . . . know?"

"Course I do, *silly*," she said, and giggled again. She stopped and pointed down the hill at a small, earthy-looking house. "Home."

She yanked his hand and he fell again. They staggered down the hill.

The house looked like it had been twisted in opposite directions from the center like a half-turned Rubik's Cube. A maple had grown through the back porch and bent over the roof. Smoke spiraled from the chimney, which was crumbling and leaning in the opposite direction of the house. The windows were glazed in a caul of ice and a shutter creaked back and forth on its hinges like an oscillating fan.

They went in.

The front door was crooked and the house shifted and bowed under his footsteps. The walls were decayed and peeling like skin. In the beams of light filtered through the tattered curtains, he saw rats crisscross on the countertops. Something dark slipped across his boot and disappeared in the shadows with liquid grace.

The little girl began to hum "This Little Light of Mine." She skipped ahead, into the living room, and said, "In here, reindeer."

"Where's your . . . mom and dad?" Skylar said. He jerked forward.

Backlit by the fire in the hearth, she giggled and sang: *"Let it shine, let it shine, le-et it shine!"*

The wind gripped the house and shook it. The shutter slammed against the sill. He jumped and looked around.

"You can sit down," she said, and he heard her moving around in the dark. He eased into a dusty chair that wobbled under his weight. She poured something, and appeared out of the shadows with a coffee mug. He watched her face—her dirt-smudged cheeks and runny nose. A missing front tooth.

She handed him the mug. "Cocoa," she said, and winked. Still humming, she slipped a moldy grey blanket around his shoulders. She stepped back into the dark.

"Your . . . parents?" he said again, his words cutting out. He cupped the mug in both hands. Felt the heat in his palms. He took a drink and his chest warmed.

"You ought not wander around out there by yourself," she said. "There's bears, ya know?"

He took a drink, never taking his eyes off her. The house shook again and popped. The shutter slammed. He pulled the blanket tight and held it under his chin. "What's your name?" he said, his voice stronger.

And she said, "Wanna hear a story?" She stoked the logs in the fire and it lit up the room.

And there it was.

Four charred spots in the floor, burned straight through the boards to the ground.

His throat went dry. Skin needled and detached from everything it held inside.

"One a ponce of the time," she said, giggling, "there was a beautiful princess—"

"This is the Otis house, ain't it?" he said, unable to take his eyes from the floor. "It's really real."

"—and one day the princess was captured by a mean ol' dragon and locked in a fiery dungeon—"

"How . . . ?" he said, and his voice was weak again.

She stepped out of the shadows, still smiling, and said, "—one day, a handsome prince arrived at the dragon's den to rescue the princess…" and a fleshy bubble pulsed and formed under her right eye, and wormed down her face. Dropped in a hot pucker mark on the floor. Her hair singed at the ends of her curls, hissed, and began to blacken in spirals to her scalp. More bubbles rose, shiny in the light, and slid off and onto the floor.

He tried to move but was frozen.

Her lips peeled back in a gap-toothed grimace. Steam wavered around her.

" . . . and he told the dragon: 'Release the princess, dragon, or face the blade of my sword!'"

He swallowed, starting to shiver. "You're . . . dead," he said, barely a whisper.

She stopped talking. Then, her voice dragging slower and slower like a damaged audiotape, said, "I'm not dead, *silly*," and disappeared.

His breath caught. He looked down and his hands were cupped, holding nothing. He looked back up and there was no house. No darkened living room or fire in the hearth. No charred floor. Only snow and thickets and trees that all looked the same.

Sitting on the ground, half-covered from the blizzard, there was not even a moldy blanket draped around him.

SOMETIME. ANYTIME.

Skylar huddled against a large oak, between its flanges that opened out into thick roots. Eyes closed. Face pale and puffy. From somewhere far away he heard the faint growl of a boat motor on the river, but he didn't open his eyes. He'd just sit awhile and wait. Stay here and rest a little longer, because he knew sometimes boats weren't boats at all. Sometimes, you heard boats like you saw old houses and little girls humming in the woods. He'd just stay here and relax, listen to the seagulls screech in the warmth of the sun. Smile at his mom and dad sitting in beach chairs behind him, laughing and sipping margaritas. Together and happy. Maybe he and his dad would toss the Frisbee along the beach. So what if that was a boat, there'd be more. There was always more. There were boats and boats, and he could sail away anytime. Toward the sun deflating into the horizon, where it watered off to somewhere, anywhere. But now, he just wanted to sit in the surf and curl his toes in the warm wet sand. Listen to the waves hiss and burst. Let the salty water foam in and over and around him, then slip silver back into the sea.

Really, it could wait.

He was warm now.

Even the shivering had stopped.

KEVIN BROWN has published two short story collections, *Death Roll* and *Ink On Wood*, and has had fiction, non-fiction, and poetry published in over 200 literary journals, magazines, and anthologies. He has won numerous writing competitions and was nominated for multiple prizes and awards, including three *Pushcart Prizes* and *The Best American Short Stories*. He co-wrote the film *Living Dark*, which won a *Moondance Film Festival Award* and was sold to New Films International, and collaborated on a television pilot with Linda Bloodworth (*Designing Women* Creator).

VASILISA WHO RAN

Patricia Lillie

S he's not much to look at," Papa says, "but she comes from good stock." He points to her four brothers sitting in the corner. "Her sister gave Gregor Andreyev a son."

"Ahhh, but she died doing it," Ivan Volkov says.

"True, but the boy is healthy and strong. He'll grow into a fine young man. An heir to be proud of. Gregor has his eye on this one too, you know. It never hurts to have a spare. Life is full of unpleasant surprises." Papa is proud of his haggling skills and well aware Ivan Volkov has had his share of unpleasant surprises.

She may not be the beauty her sister was, but Vasilisa knows her father intends to get a good price for his remaining daughter.

"Her housekeeping is excellent. She cooks well. She spins, she weaves. She's skilled in all the womanly arts. Her mother has made sure of it," Papa says. Mama hangs her head.

"There is only one womanly art I am interested in," Ivan Volkov says. "I want a son. I have servants for the rest."

In her father's house, Vasilisa is the servant, but she's heard the talk. Ivan Volkov has tried to plant a son in more than one house maid, willing or not. Better a servant in her father's house than a sacrifice in Ivan Volkov's.

"Again, good stock," Papa says.

Her brothers stand. Tall, strong, handsome. Anyone would be proud to call them family. There is no doubt one will bring home a bride to care for Mama and Papa in their old age. Vasilisa is expendable, worth only as much as Ivan Volkov is willing to give. Despite what Papa said about Gregor Andreyev, she's had no other suitors. Papa isn't above lying to get what he wants.

Her father grabs her arm and drags her before Ivan Volkov. He is not a large man. Vasilisa towers over him. She draws herself tall and looks down her long nose at him. He will not like that. He steps back and examines her from head to toe, like a horse in the market. He stops short of pulling back her lips and examining her teeth. He sniggers at the toes of her large brown boots peeking from beneath the hem of her skirt.

"Do you want to be married?" he says.

"Not to you."

Her parents' gasps suck the air from the room. One of her

brothers snickers. Angry purple flushes Ivan Volkov's face. His eyes narrow. A thick, ugly vein throbs in his neck. She waits for him to strike her.

No one speaks to Ivan Volkov in such a tone.

Instead, he laughs. A dry, mocking laugh that tells her exactly what she means to him. A laugh that tells her she will pay for her insolence. A laugh that contains her entire future.

"I'll take her," he says.

He and Papa shake hands and slap each other on the back. They leave for the inn, where they will negotiate the terms of the marriage over food and drink. Mostly the latter.

It is done. Vasilisa will become Ivan Volkov's fourth wife.

VASILISA WASN'T MUCH more than a toddler when Ivan Volkov's first marriage took place. She doesn't remember his first wife, but the grandmothers still tell the story—behind Ivan Volkov's back, of course.

The wedding was magnificent, as befitting the union of the village's most important and influential man—he was reputed to be a distant relation of the Tsar—to the most beautiful woman to ever grace the village.

Before the year was out, Anna Levedeva's belly swelled. Ivan Volkov strutted like a rooster.

"My son will be brilliant and bold. He will grow up to marry a

Tsarevna," he boasted.

Both mother and infant survived the birth, but not the night.

"It was the oddest thing," the midwife said. "That little girl had hair the color of a carrot."

Neither Ivan Volkov nor Anna Levedeva had red hair. No one in the village had red hair. The grandmothers examined the lineage of both Volkov and Levedeva but couldn't come up with a single redhead.

The only red hair they knew of belonged to an itinerant scholar who'd passed through the village less than a year—but more than a half year—earlier. He'd stayed a month before moving on to better things.

Ivan Volkov buried his wife and daughter and moved on to better things himself.

HER FATHER RETURNS.

"The wedding will be in two weeks." He slurs his words.

"But that's no time! Her dress, her trousseau. The wedding feast . . . " Mama looks as if she is about to cry.

"We will provide the bride. Her new husband will provide everything else," Papa says. He staggers off to bed and shouts for Mama to follow. She obeys.

Vasilisa is left alone. Papa has gotten rid of her and at no cost to himself, unless he paid for Ivan Volkov's drinks. She hopes she was worth at least the cost of a decent vodka and wonders what Ivan Volkov promised in return. Vasilisa's eyes burn, but her tears are of rage, not sorrow.

IVAN VOLKOV'S SECOND wedding wasn't as grand as his first, nor was his second wife as beautiful as her predecessor. Vasilisa remembers her. Marya Romanovna was delighted to be elevated from a simple farmer's daughter to the wife of a rich and powerful man. She flaunted her new wealth and lorded her position over her fellow villagers every chance she got.

Neither her position nor her pride did her any good. After four years with no sign of a pregnancy, she fell ill. The wasting disease destroyed what little beauty she had within a week. She was dead within two.

"Such a tragedy," the grandmothers said. All of Ivan Volkov's money and connections couldn't buy him a son. It didn't stop him from trying.

After a suitable period of mourning—depending on one's definition of suitable—he left the village and brought back a bride from outside. This one was quiet and meek. She stared at the ground, never looked anyone in the eye, and barely spoke above a whisper. Two years later, she was found floating in the river. Vasilisa doesn't remember her name, if she ever knew it.

Ivan Volkov still didn't have his heir.

The village children invented a new game. One was the "Ivan" who chased the others. *If the Ivan catches you, you are his bride. If the Ivan catches you, you are dead.*

"I WANT TO live," Vasilisa says.

"Then you'd better give him a son," Mama says.

"I won't."

"You have no choice."

But she does.

VASILISA CREEPS FROM her bed and dresses in silence. She wraps herself in a cloak the color of midnight and carries her boots. Her father's house hums around her, breathing in rhythm with its sleeping occupants. She hunches over and makes herself as small as possible. Tiptoeing in her stocking feet to avoid the creaky floorboards, she makes her way to the door.

She pauses to put on her boots. Her mother appears beside her.

Mama places her finger to her lips and tucks something into Vasilisa's pocket. She leans close and whispers in Vasilisa's ear. Words Vasilisa knows. Words everyone knows. Words that, until now, have only been a silly children's chant. *Little house, little house, turn your face to me and your back to the forest.*

Her mother knows where she is going.

"Follow the river," Mama whispers.

Vasilisa opens her mouth to speak, to tell her mother goodbye, to tell her she loves her despite everything, but Mama places her hand over Vasilisa's mouth. "Run," she says and unbolts the door.

Vasilisa runs.

THREE MARES WAIT in Papa's stable, one white, one red, one black. Vasilisa chooses the black. She may not be the fastest, but she will blend into the night.

"No." Her youngest brother stops her as she lifts a saddle to the mare's back. Of all her brothers, Dmitri has always been the kind one.

"Please," she says.

"Papa."

She understands. Papa will not lament the loss of a daughter—unless Ivan Volkov offered far more than even she thinks she's worth—but a stolen horse he will hunt to the ends of the earth.

Dmitri saddles the mare and pulls Vasilisa up behind him. Together, they ride into the night.

He takes her to the place where the forest meets the river.

"Be safe," he says and turns for home.

She slips her hand into her pocket, thinking Mama has provided food for her journey. She finds a small wooden doll. It belonged to Mama and to her mother before her. Mama's treasure, never a toy for clumsy little girls. Vasilisa has never been allowed to hold it. She is touched by the gift, but bread would have been more useful.

She enters the forest and follows the river.

THE TREES ARE full of women. Their green hair flutters in a breeze that isn't there. Their long pale arms reach for her, and she knows there is comfort in their embrace. Safety.

No. That is not what she's come for. Not what she wants.

"Join us, Vasilisa," the Rusalki croon. Their song promises peace. Belonging. Things Vasilisa has never known.

She sways.

"Join us."

She closes her eyes. The river calls.

She puts her hand in her pocket and wraps her fingers around the doll. *Resist.* The doll grows warm. *Resist.* She hears the word not with her ears, but in her bones. The cries of the Rusalki fade.

When she opens her eyes, three Rusalki block her way. One holds a baby wrapped in a blanket. One stares at the ground.

The third twists her face into a sneer. "Why should you be the one to live?" she says.

Vasilisa grasps the doll.

"*Do not answer.*"

"Why you and not us?"

"*Do not answer.*"

"What makes you different?"

Vasilisa remains silent.

"No. You *are* different. Not one of us." The Rusalka slumps, beaten and dejected.

Vasilisa moves to reach out, to comfort her. This welling of sympathy is a new feeling. She's not sure she likes it.

"*Resist,*" the doll says.

She backs away.

Marya Romanovna gathers her arrogance around her like armor. Her pupilless eyes flash. "Were you followed?" she says.

"Vasilisa!" A shout in the distance. A man. Papa? "You can't hide!" No. Ivan Volkov.

"Run," the chorus of Rusalki shrieks.

Vasilisa runs.

SHE IS EXHAUSTED. Her head aches and her feet scream with blisters. She sinks to the ground.

The Rusalki no longer beckon her to join them.

"Get up. Go on," the trees whisper.

"*Listen,*" the doll says.

She gets up and takes a painful step forward.

SHE STUMBLES INTO a clearing as the sun comes up. She's reached her destination, but it's all wrong. Where she expected to find a tall fence topped with skulls, only bent and broken spikes remain. The iron gate stands open, rusty and half off its hinges. Dusty and dry chicken legs buckle under the weight of the hut they hold. Fallen shingles litter the small yard. The windows are dark. The house does not turn its back to her. It is empty. Dead.

She can run no farther. She wants to crawl into the house and die there with it, but the door is high above her head, out of reach. If she lies down in the yard, Ivan Volkov will find her. Either way, she's as dead as the witch's house.

She reaches into her pocket and clutches the doll.

"*Say it.*"

She doesn't understand. The words her mother gave her are useless. The house is still, its dark, closed face already turned toward her.

"*Say it.*"

"Little house, little house, turn your face to me and your back to the forest," she says.

Something flickers in the windows. Or else she's so tired her eyes are playing tricks on her.

"*Say it again.*"

She does. Another flicker, and the hut lights up.

"*Again.*"

Once more, Vasilisa repeats the chant.

The front door opens and slams shut. A ladder unfurls.

The gate screeches when she lifts it back onto its hinges and closes it behind her. The rotted rope of the ladder doesn't look as if it will hold her weight, but she has nothing to lose. She climbs.

She knocks at the door, once, twice, three times. No one answers. She tries the latch, but it is frozen. The door is locked.

Above the latch, the weathered wood of the door quivers and comes alive. A mouth takes shape. Black lips part, and the mouth opens wide to reveal row after row of razor-sharp metal teeth waiting to be fed.

A lock, but she doesn't have a key.

"*Use me*," the wooden doll says.

She takes Mama's treasure from her pocket and cradles it in cupped hands. "Thank you, Mama," she whispers and kisses the silent doll.

She inserts the doll into the gaping mouth. The teeth snap shut, and she is left clutching two little wooden legs. Her mother's screams echo inside her head. The door swings open. She enters the witch's house and falls to her knees.

She is too late.

Giant bones stretch from one corner of the hut to the other. A skull rests near the oven. Next to a large mortar and pestle, oversized feet point to the ceiling. There will be no help for her here, and she is beyond caring.

Vasilisa curls up on the floor, nestled inside the dead baba yaga's ribs. As she drifts off, she imagines she hears a voice.

"*Sister*," the bones say.

SHE SLEEPS THROUGH the day and into the night. When she awakes, the bones have crumbled. The wooden doll, whole again, lies half buried in the coarse grey dust. She puts it in her pocket. Without knowing why, she dips her finger in the dust and puts it in her mouth. The house trembles.

Outside, something shrieks. *The gate. Ivan Volkov has found her.*

The shriek becomes a chorus, and the chorus becomes a song.

She goes to the window. Moonlight gleams on pale skin. The Rusalki have come. They fill the clearing, far more of them than she remembers.

She opens the door, and the Rusalki fall silent. Three women step forward. One cradles a carrot-headed baby. One lifts her face to the stars and smiles. Marya Romanovna holds a severed head. She raises it high and thrusts it down onto a jagged fencepost. The house quivers and moans. The Rusalki bow in unison and back away.

A black cloud descends from the sky. By the time the crows have done their work, the Rusalki are gone, back to their river and trees. On the fencepost, a skull—all that is left of Ivan Volkov—gleams in the moonlight.

THE HOUSE CREAKS. It tilts to one side, then the other. It shakes itself awake. It spins and dances.

Vasilisa sweeps up the remains of the last baba yaga and fills a glass jar with the dust. She places it on a shelf amid a long line of similar jars filled with similar dust. Someday, she will join them.

But not yet.

PATRICIA LILLIE grew up in a haunted house in a small town in Northeast Ohio. Since then, she has published picture books, short stories, fonts, and novels. Her short story collection, *The Cuckoo Girls*, was a 2020 Bram Stoker Award finalist. Her novels include *The Ceiling Man* and *Ghosts in Glass Houses* (written as Kay Charles). Lillie teaches in Southern New Hampshire University's MFA in Creative Writing program. She also knits, sometimes purls, and can be found on Twitter @patricialillie.

A LOVE SO DEEP

Christian Riley

T his isn't San Diego, Claire. That weather is long gone, I'm
afraid."

It was Alaskan weather. Southeastern, to be precise, and Walter's
old bones now felt the chill every day of the year. Presently, he sat
in his skiff and tugged on a wet rope, pulling his shrimp pot up
from the frigid seafloor. A chilly breeze and rolling wave idled past,
sending the small boat into a gentle pitch. Walter paused momen-
tarily to catch his balance. Blinking his eyes, he felt a sudden itch
deep inside his throat, coughed, then hawked phlegm overboard.
He stared hauntingly at it, watching as the pinkish-green glob rode
the water's surface for a few seconds, like a jellyfish, before its weight
dragged it down.

"You might . . . like it here," Walter stammered. He continued to pull on the rope, bringing the pot up. He pursed his lips and squinted, the sea mist batting at his eyes. "Sure, it's cold. Real cold. You wouldn't like any of that. But by gosh, it's pretty . . . "

The pot came up loaded, a few dozen shrimp kicking and bucking en masse inside the cage. Walter blinked and dumped the catch into a plastic box beside him. He re-baited the pot, tossed it back into the water, then looked up as it sank. The shoreline was only a hundred yards away, pine-laden stretches with deep black hollows and eerie shadows, countless miles of conifers as far as the eye can see. Bears, wolves, and wolverines roamed this world, Walter knew. He'd seen at least one of those animals every week since living up here. Occasionally, he also wondered about the animals rarely seen, the myths and legends that lurked in the woods or in the ocean. People talked about them. Walter knew that as well.

The pot now settled, he tossed the anchoring buoy out and away and then puttered onward. His skiff was an aluminum fishing boat with a Yamaha outboard motor. Nothing special, just your standard transportation for the area. He'd purchased the boat from a dealer over in Juneau during his first months as an Alaskan resident. That was over three years ago. And now Walter lived alone in a cabin near Petersburg, his nearest neighbor a good twenty minutes by boat.

"Mighty pretty, darling." He coughed again, approaching the next shrimp pot.

It had taken Walter a while to get things figured out these last few years. At sixty-eight, he'd been retired for almost a decade, leaving the workforce early, thanks to his pension. Being retired for so long, he was used to keeping himself busy. Especially when he'd had Claire to share his time with. But like a burglar in the night, cancer robbed Walter of his wife, and then he didn't know what to do with himself. In time, he'd become a lost soul, a rudderless boat set adrift in a wild and terrible sea.

"It's wet, and it's cold, but golly-gee-willikers … Yeah, it's pretty, Claire."

There had been nothing up here for him. Nothing but a bleak patchwork of ocean and forest. It was all new, all forbidden and merciless, not a helping soul in sight. With no children, and then no wife, and all but a few distant friends, Walter viewed his move to Alaska as sort of his final rest stop, a last step back to the primordial den before the night came on. And it would be the place he would learn to live in now, for however long such time would keep him—months, years, who knew?—before he too succumbed to the call of death. Then again, maybe that time would be less than expected. Months, years, or perhaps just days. Walter's next cough was a dreadful one, producing half a mouthful of phlegm over the gunwale.

He watched as the sea pulled his dying self to the bottom. *Would a fish eat at it?* he wondered. Would the shrimp and crabs feast on his inner-scab, like they did with all the other carnage?

Despite his ailments, Walter still had his appetite. The bounty of the land helped with that. He fished regularly, damn near daily. He fished for shrimp and salmon, halibut, crab, and cod, various rockfish and other seafood, gathered clams from off the beach, all of which he consumed with delight. It tickled him, knowing that for just a few hours out on the water or combing the shoreline, Walter could come home with several top-dollar meals. He hunted the land as well, for deer and small game, but that was less frequent, and often less productive, yet more laborious, as it was hard on his knees. Hunting was a chore.

Moments later, the second pot was over the rail and into the pale, slick as grease. Another load of shrimp. Two days' worth, maybe more. He re-baited this pot as well, threw it over the side, then trolled along. He had one more to check, and then Walter figured he'd do a little fishing before calling it quits for the day.

The third and last pot was the heaviest. Walter grunted as he manipulated the basket into the boat. A hundred kicking shrimp, probably more. He dumped the load into the box, threw it back out, and moments later was heading toward a cluster of rocks he liked to fish at. When he arrived, Walter cut the engine, dropped anchor, and then stared at his boots for three honest minutes.

He did this all the time now. That's how it seemed, at least. He wasn't sure how often, and certainly had no clue why, but every day Walter found himself caught in some thousand-yard stare for minutes on end. And perhaps the worst of it was that during these fugue moments, not a damn thing went through Walter's head, other than the image of what he was looking at.

Another cough, and the Zen-like dreaminess shattered. Walter looked up, and with movements that appeared robotic, he retrieved his fishing pole, secured it with a drop lure, then put the tackle over the side of the boat and released the spool.

"You'd like the food, Claire, oh wouldn't you," he said. "Every bit of it. Remember how you loved to go to Top of the Market? Lord, their halibut was dandy." Walter chuckled, then glanced at the squirming mass of critters in the box next to him. "I got it all right here, Claire. All of it . . . And it's practically free."

A sudden, violent yank down on his pole, and then Walter joined the fray, cranking hard on the reel. It was a giant, he could tell, so he reached quickly for the gaff. Several seconds later here it was, up on the surface, a twenty-pound halibut, if was an ounce. With one quick swing, Walter rammed the gaff into the fish's side, then huffed as he lugged it over the gunwale. He blinked in awe, looked at the fish, at his boots, then the fish again. "You see, Claire," he said with a faltering smile, "it's all right here." Then Walter broke into a raspy cough.

LATER THAT NIGHT, the old man ate like a king. Baked halibut with steamed shrimp, a stick's worth of butter drowning the whole affair. He stuffed himself silly and washed it all down with three beers, then sat in the kitchen and listened to the pattering rain outside. "Goddamit, woman," he whispered after some time, wiping tears from his eyes. "Why, oh, why? Just why?"

Good morning, my love. How about we get coffee in Seaport Village?

"Claire? Is that you . . . ?"

Then we can take an early walk. Or maybe breakfast in Coronado. Whatever you'd like. We've got the whole day, hun. No . . . We've got the rest of our lives.

"Claire!"

Walter lifted out of his sleep and into the darkness of his cabin. He blinked with confusion, peering at the shadows, and slowly realized the error of his mind. Fooled again, he was. Fooled by his own dream. And then the dream gave way to the reality of his living nightmare, that dreadful feeling of being so, so alone.

Walter lied back down, but then started hacking terribly, which forced him to get up out of bed and stagger to the bathroom, where he turned on the light then hawked the night's worth of death into the shower. A wet scab of green and brown and pink, all sliding down the drain. Walter gagged, then spat some more, before wiping his mouth on a towel. Then he sat on the toilet and looked at his unkempt toenails. She used to trim those things for him, weird as that was. But what married couple didn't have a fetish or two? The nails were ragged now, just like Walter's lungs, and like his toiling thoughts, and who knew what else.

He made it out of the bathroom and into the kitchen, and some-time later, out into the cold morning air, where he sat on a chair with coffee in hand, looking out at the glassy surface of Frederick Sound. The sun was up, but it was concealed by a heavy layer of fog. The temperature was a brisk forty-seven degrees. The salty mist from the sea lingered in the dead air. Walter could taste it on his lips. The flavor went well with the dark roast he was drinking.

"Maybe I'll check on them pots early, before the rain picks up again. How's that sound to you, Claire?"

Walter finished his coffee, used the bathroom, then dressed in his slickers and went outside. His fishing boat was tied to a weathered dock less than twenty feet from his front door. He climbed into it and looked over the gunwale, down into the murky water below. The bay was deep, and on mornings like this, foggy as it was, no way in hell could he see the bottom. But Walter looked anyway. He always looked. Then he sat back, retrieved a plastic jug he kept secured to the boat, and preceded to bail out a good amount of rainwater.

It took a few minutes, and during this time Walter thought about how cold and wet and dreary his new world was. It was always like this, every goddamn day of the year, even worse in the winter, and old Walter never could figure out why he'd picked such a miserable place to end his life in.

He glanced over the gunwale again. "Where does it go?" he said, thinking about how final the black depths below looked. "In the end where does love go, Claire? Where did *your* love go?"

AN HOUR LATER, Walter was pulling up his third shrimp pot, the last pot of the day, when he felt a massive tug on the line. Startled, the old man paused, wondering what the heck had just happened. He recommenced with pulling, then there it came again, a second tug, only much stronger. Wondering if it was a sea lion trying to rob him of his bounty, Walter pulled on the line frantically. The tugging continued, as fierce as the halibut fight the day before—but over a shrimp pot?

Studying the end of his rope, Walter fought and pulled, until he could see the top rim of the cage just below the surface. The whole thing was shaking fiercely now. The fight was raging and, curious as hell, Walter leaned forward and peered into the water.

Immediately, the tugging stopped. And then Walter caught a glimpse, just before it swam away. He saw its face, pale green, oval shaped, with long black tendrils of—hair?—flailing limply in the current. And then, of course, the eyes.

Walter gasped, then scanned the surrounding water before sitting back down. He almost drowned in the quagmire of his thoughts, but several minutes later he finally looked up and said, "Claire?"

IT RAINED LIKE hell that night. As he cooked another shrimp

and halibut dinner, Walter stood in his kitchen and gazed out the window, staring at the abyss outside. The world before him was black as the grave, not a hint of light anywhere. He could kill all that if he wanted to. All Walter had to do was walk over to the door, flip the switch to the porch and dock lights, then see for himself.

He did that sometimes, when the rain and the wind worked together, thick as thieves, because sometimes the feeling that came over him when he saw such swirling madness was the coziest feeling he'd ever felt. But not tonight. No. Walter just stood and stared into the blackened universe, until his dinner was ready, and he was then sitting by candlelight at his dining table, chewing away.

It was another fine meal, fresh as the one from the night before, a full plate of protein to feed his dying body. Walter had cooked everything to perfection, just the right amount of time to keep the halibut and shrimp juicy, not dry, not rubbery. He smiled at his accomplishment, was truly satisfied . . . for the moment, at least.

"You'd like this," he said, frowning. "It tastes splendid. Tastes like . . . maybe . . . our first meal together."

Outside, the wind died down, and the rain let up. Walter heard the water running down his gutters, heard it splashing onto his front deck, a torrent from heaven to earth right there above his head. "It's amazing how much this place has to offer, Claire. I think you'd love it."

Yes, Walter. Yes, I would.

What was that? Walter's eyes widened. He set his fork down, looked at his front door, and listened. "Claire?"

I would.

"Claire . . . !"

Walter pushed his chair back and stood. Then he staggered to the door and opened it, felt the frigid blast of air. He saw only darkness, so he flipped the light switch. There was nothing there—of course, there was nothing. Just a river of water tumbling off his roof, and the wet and weathered slats of his front porch. Nothing there at all . . .

Two minutes later, Walter realized he'd been staring at a shiny streak of muck on the ground in front of him. It had started at his front door, and trailed outward, down the steps and onto the dock, where it then cut sharply, disappearing at the water's edge. It looked like tar, thick and black, impervious to the rain's onslaught, and glistening vaguely in the night, as if dusted lightly with diamonds.

WALTER KEPT THE photo albums in the spare bedroom, stashed in a box underneath a table. The pain of looking through his past life was so great, it might as well have been terminal. The last time he looked, in fact, was on their anniversary, a year ago. Walter cried dreadfully that night, cried himself to sleep. And when he woke up, that's when he first felt the itch deep inside his throat. The cough came a few months after, and things had only gotten worse from there.

But on this night, the night of the torrential rainstorm, followed by her voice, and then that curious black trail, Walter pulled the box out from under the table. He sat on his couch and flipped through the albums, screening randomly through the years at first, but then taking a systematic approach after. Year by year, from start to finish, all the frozen moments of happiness and love, until finally the end, with the empty pages glaring back at him. *This is all that's left of you, old man*, he thought. *Nothing but empty pages. Nothing but dead pages.*

The rain picked up again, and then Walter blinked and looked at the clock. Half-past two. As if that mattered any. Where was he supposed to be in the morning? What job did he have waiting for him? What urgent errand needed to get done? Walter sighed, knowing that the answers to those questions were a mirror reflection of the remainder of his photo albums. There was not one thing—not one person—left in this world that needed anything from him anymore. Not one thing at all.

Even so, Walter set the albums aside and meandered off to bed, hacking intermittently as he drifted to sleep.

SOMETIME LATER, in the dark, the old man stood in the corner of his bedroom, crying. He couldn't remember how or why he'd gotten there, but he knew what he was thinking now, with the barrel of his .45 pressed against his temple.

Don't do it, Walter.

"I have to, Claire. I just have to."

Please don't. Not now . . . Not yet.

A FEW MORNINGS later, Walter was out at sea. The pots were especially heavy coming up. He hacked and grunted and bled a trail of crimson from his mouth as he got them up and over the rail. Two pots full of desperately squirming critters, now several days' worth of sustenance for the old man.

He thought about this as he pulled on the third pot. And he thought about that thing he'd seen a few days earlier, just under the water, fighting him for a meal, with that look in her eyes . . .

When he got the pot over the rail, Walter opened the cage door and then flipped the pot over, back into the water. He grabbed it and shook it roughly, watching as the critters poured out, and as the pot emptied. He wondered how far down they went before something—before *she* gobbled them up.

HE COULDN'T REMEMBER eating that night, but he'd done so anyway. It was another blustery day followed by a downpour for an evening, and long into the darkness, the old man found himself sitting on the couch with a full belly, staring quizzically at his hands. They were covered with cuts and scratches, abrasions, skinned knuckles . . . all the normal wear and tear that came with living in this dreadfully beautiful wilderness. "You would love it here," he whispered hopelessly, looking then at the table, and at the plate of food he'd left for her. *That's right*, he thought, staring at the pile of shrimp, lathered now in cold butter. *That's what I ate.*

And Walter couldn't remember taking a shower later that night, and then getting into his bed, his wracking cough being the one thing to bring him back to the painful present. "I'm dying without you, Claire," he mumbled, crawling into the covers, then falling fast asleep.

You are not without me, Walter.

And then later she made sweet love to him, in the cold and murky night, the slithering of her wet body bringing with it a moist warmness, suctioning sounds, and a brackish aroma, the entire sultry moment of passion drowning Walter with the feelings he'd been missing for so damn long.

THE NEXT MORNING, Walter staggered out of bed and to the bathroom, where he coughed half his lungs out and into the toilet. The color and thickness of his discharge were a frightening sight. Walter flushed the toilet, then got up and made his way to the kitchen. He wondered about the night, and if that was a dream he'd had . . .

Of course, it was a dream.

But then he saw her plate on the table, and it was empty, completely empty, no shrimp tails or butter residue, nothing at all.

The plate had been licked clean.

Walter looked around, bewildered. The room was filled with a salty odor, but that wasn't particularly uncommon. He checked the door, found that it wasn't locked. And that too wasn't uncommon, because out here, Walter rarely, if ever, locked his house.

Even so . . .

Hesitating, he poured himself some coffee, then went outside and stood on the porch, noticing that *yes*, the trail was there again—a long black streak leading down to the water's edge. Mesmerized, Walter stared at that trail for what felt like half the morning. He really didn't know how long, but his coffee was cold by the time he finally looked away.

The black streak he'd been staring at reflected the sky above, for another thick storm had moved in from the sea. A sudden gust of wind blew violently past Walter, the force so strong that he grabbed the porch railing to steady himself. And as the wind screamed by, the old man swore he heard his wife's voice again.

You are not without me, Walter.

"I am not without you," Walter whispered. Then he dropped his coffee cup onto the porch and staggered down to the dock. "I'm coming, darling," he said, climbing into his boat. There were a few inches of water in the skiff, but Walter didn't bother with bailing. And he didn't look down, over the gunwale, either . . . For once, he didn't look down.

"I'm coming, darling," he repeated, firing up the boat's motor.

And the wind and the rain raged against him, thick as thieves they were, as he left the bay and cruised out to sea. The sky was now a pool of shadow, a slate of grey reflecting the forbidden land and depressing water, all of which had become the miserable embodiment of Walter's life. "I'm coming," he mumbled desperately, blinking at the storm as he moved on.

He was soaked by the time he arrived. It was here that he first saw her, Walter was sure. He was clutching the gunwale now, the storm-wrought waves tossing his boat like a toy in a bathtub. Walter peered overboard, stared at the cold depths for a long minute.

"You're down there, aren't you, darling? You're down there, just waiting for me."

There were several inches in the boat now, sloshing back and forth across Walter's ankles, mimicking the surrounding waves. But Walter didn't care. No, he didn't care anymore.

Yes, I'm down here . . .

And that was the final straw. Walter took hold of his anchor, tied it to his waist, then dove overboard. At once, the storm disappeared, replaced by a fierce chill. The ice-cold grip of the ocean squeezed at Walter's lungs, and it was all he could do to fight off his dying cough, all the way down, through ten fathoms of bitter sea until at last, the old man reached the bottom.

It was quiet now, he realized . . . His entire world had become deathly quiet, a most amazing sound. *I'm here, my wife,* Walter thought, staring curiously at the shrouded veil surrounding him. *I'm here, darling*, he thought again, wondering when that beautiful woman would finally return to him her long-lost love. *I'm here . . .* he almost muttered, the mask of death swimming toward him now, coming out of the shadows, with those big, hungry eyes.

Wait . . . that's not you, Claire, Walter thought—his final thought. And then, at last, the darkness took him.

CHRISTIAN RILEY lives near Sacramento, California, vowing one day to move back to the Pacific Northwest. In the meantime, he teaches special education, writes cool stories, and hides from the blasting heat for six months of the year. He has had over 100 short stories published in various magazines and anthologies, and across various genres. He is the author of the literary suspense novels *The Sinking of the Angie Piper* and *The Broken Pines*. For more information, go to www.chrisrileyauthor.com.

ABOUT THE EDITOR

C.M. MULLER lives in St. Paul, Minnesota with his wife and two sons—and, of course, all those quaint and curious volumes of forgotten lore. He is related to the Norwegian writer Jonas Lie and draws much inspiration from that scrivener of old. His tales have appeared in *Shadows & Tall Trees*, *Dim Shores*, *Vastarien*, and a host of other venues. He has published two collections of his short fiction: *Hidden Folk* (2018) and *Secondary Roads* (2022).

CHTHONIC MATTER
PUBLICATIONS

If you enjoyed these darkside tales, and need a further fictional fix, don't hesitate to check out the many other publications found under the Chthonic Matter imprint:

<u>NIGHTSCRIPT</u> : An 8-Volume Anthology

<u>TWICE-TOLD</u> : A Collection of Doubles

<u>OCULUS SINISTER</u> : An Anthology of Ocular Horror

<u>COME OCTOBER</u> : An Anthology of Autumnal Horror

For more information, please visit:

www.chthonicmatter.wordpress.com

www.chthonicmatter.wordpress.com

Made in the USA
Monee, IL
24 March 2023

30249118R00081